For

Ava_____

Not a Fairytale

Love

Shaidq

Not a Fairytale

SHAIDA KAZIE ALI

UMUZI

Published in 2010 by Umuzi
an imprint of Random House Struik (Pty) Ltd
Company Reg No 1966/003153/07
80 McKenzie Street, Cape Town 8001, South Africa
PO Box 1144, Cape Town 8000, South Africa
umuzi@randomstruik.co.za
www.umuzi-randomhouse.co.za

First edition, first printing 2010

1 3 5 7 9 8 6 4 2

ISBN 978-1-4152-0112-1

Cover design by Mallemeule
Text design by Chérie Collins
Set in 11.5 on 14 pt Garamond Pro
Printed and bound by Interpak Books, Pietermaritzburg

For Nuri, phoenix

The truth will set you free. But first, it will piss you off.
GLORIA STEINEM

Contents

Once upon a time there were two sisters, Salena and Zuhra. If this were a fairytale, there'd have been three: the older two ugly and avaricious, the younger one beautiful and kind. (She's the one who'd get the prince.) But this is no fairytale, so two is all you're going to get.

When pale-skinned Salena was born, her father's eye happened to fall on the new moon outside the bedroom window as he was trying to find a name for her. Older by ten years, Salena is shy and silent while Zuhra (the father again turned to the night sky for inspiration – Venus this time), when her nose is not stuffed in a book, wields her tongue like a cheese grater. Where her sister is fair and malleable, she is dark and wild haired and resolute.

But I'll let Zuhra tell you her story – her words are better than mine, or so she thinks.

Zuhra's Tale

Under the Counter

I'M SITTING UNDER THE COUNTER IN PAPA'S SHOP sniffing paraffin from a small drum and hoping a customer will come along soon. Even though I'm only five it's my job to pump the paraffin into their bottles. I love the smell and I love filling the customers' bottles. It makes me feel like I'm a big girl.

I don't like the smell of the purple stuff the dronkies buy with half a loaf of white bread, though I'd like to taste that pretty colour. But Papa won't even let me hold the bottle. He says it's poisonous.

Sometimes when Papa's busy counting money I'll steal a sweet or bubblegum. I love Chappies and Wicks and the sticky red sweets without a name. But my favourite thing of all is Disprin. Papa says it's medicine and I'm not allowed to eat it, but as soon as he and my sister Salena are busy serving customers, I take one out of its pretty silver and blue wrapping and pop it in my mouth. It melts on my tongue with small sparks like bright lights going on and off.

When I'm not pumping paraffin or helping myself to sweets I wait for the regular customers to play with me. There's the tattoo man from next door who doesn't have any skin that isn't blue or green or red. Mrs Tattoo has long straight black hair and she's always trying to comb mine with her hands so it will lie flat, but it never does. Across the road are the Levines, who have eleven children. Every day they buy bread and milk and tea on the book, although I've never seen them bring in a book. Papa says if they ever pay back all the money they owe him he'll be very very rich. Mrs Levine chats to Ma a lot. She's supposed to be coloured, but she's trying to get a white card because of her children. Some of them are fair like Salena and have green eyes like hers, but the others are even darker than me.

A white card means you are white like Mrs Cloete, with her rain-grey bun and mouse-brown skin, who lives on top of the shop. If she sees me walking on the pavement outside our shop, she screams at me to get off it because pavements are for whites and not Indian Bushmen like me. Once she even threw her pee-pot down on Salena and me when we were walking home, screaming, "Af vannie pavement!" Luckily it missed us. Salena stood there and stared up at her till Mrs Cloete went inside and smashed her balcony door closed. I ran home to tell Ma and she got that scary look on her face. I was hoping she'd give Mrs Cloete a hiding but she did nothing.

I like the customers, but my best friends are my two cats. They're supposed to catch rats in the shop and the house, but really they're my walking dollies. Tommy-Tiger (named after a bubblegum we sell in the shop) is grey with black stripes. He's the oldest, even older than me. He loves packets of salt 'n vinegar chips from the shop. And then there's my favourite, Ginger. He is dark orange and has a pretty pink smile. He shares my blankie with me, and on the nights when he stays out late I can't sleep.

Every day I go into the pet-food shop with a silver ten-cent piece Ma gives me and I ask for "tencentshorseminceplease". The man in his white coat with red marks on it gives me the parcel in white paper and I take it home to the cats, and they eat it on the kitchen floor. I love them so much.

Sometimes I spend Saturday mornings at the Gem bioscope with Salena, and now and then our brother, Faruk-Paruk, comes with us, if he's not helping Papa in the shop. I like the Tom and Jerry cartoons, but I wish Tom could beat that mouse. Tom gets hit over and over and those pink bumps grow and grow on his head. I know that doesn't happen in real life because I've seen the marks on Salena's body after Papa has beaten her and they're usually purple and green like Chappies. The Gem is dark and smoky and smells of fish and chips. It makes me feel warm and cosy and I don't even mind the cockroaches.

Moving

One day Salena goes to OK Bazaars in town to buy Ma some material, but while she is gone the police phone Ma to come pick her up at Caledon Square. They took her there because she was holding hands with a dark-skinned boy in the Gardens. They want Ma to prove that she's Indian, because they think she looks white.

Ma grabs me and we go off to the bus stop just outside the shop. First she tells Papa where she's going. He looks so cross, I know Salena's going to get another hiding. We have to wait a long time for our bus, and by the time it comes Ma is so angry she looks like Tommy-Tiger when he gets wet.

At the police station Ma first screams at the boy (I don't know his name) and then she takes out her green ID card to show the police. Salena is crying quietly, the way she does everything. She doesn't say a word. And when we get home, Ma locks her in our bedroom.

That night I lie on the floor in the front room and listen to Ma and Papa. They have decided it is time to find a husband for Salena, before she brings shame to the family.

On Monday the postman brings a fat letter in a brown envelope that says we must get out of Woodstock. The letter says we can keep the shop because a white lady owns it, but we can't live in our house. They have got a house for us in an Indian area, and we have to move to a place called Cravenby.

We move very soon and I am sorry to go. Even the cats don't like the new house. Tommy-Tiger goes missing and two weeks later he turns up at the shop in Woodstock. Ma rubs butter on his paws and says that will stop him from running away again.

Now there are new neighbours for me to get to know, and soon I have names for all of them. On our right is Motjie Curry – when you walk pass her house you can always smell chicken or fish curry cooking. She came straight from the village in India and she's been in the area since before I was born. On the left is a dark-skinned man with a big red "L" on his car, because he is a learner driver, Faruk-Paruk tells me. So I call him Mr Learner and his wife Mrs Learner. Next to him is Mrs Koeksister, a Malay woman married to an Indian man. She looks like a big koeksister that's been left in the syrup too long, dark and shiny with white hair like coconut sprinkles. Across the road are three houses filled with The Gossipers: three women (married to three brothers) who chat to each other over their fences.

The new house has wooden floors, and every morning I wake up to hear Ma's shoes clickety-clacking on the floor and her telling Salena what to clean for the day. The house is too big for Salena to clean on her own, so Ma hires a servant, Gladys. Ma gets Gladys a special plate and cup and saves all the leftover food for her. But Gladys doesn't stay long. When I ask Ma why Gladys left, she gets one of her looks and says nothing. I think Ma's cross because she caught Faruk-Paruk kissing Gladys. Imagine having to kiss Faruk-Paruk, like that princess who had to kiss a frog. Yuck!

Snap, Crackle, Pop!

THERE ARE ALL KINDS OF ANIMALS that live around the new house. It's very different from Woodstock, where there were just mice and rats and cockroaches. Here there are lizards, frogs, locusts, chameleons, spiders and lots of birds. I'm scared of the lizards and the way they can spit off their tails, which carry on wriggling even when they're not on their bodies anymore. Faruk-Paruk catches the lizards and tortures them. He stuffs them into empty milk bottles and throws petrol over them, then burns them with matches. He forces me to watch. He says it's for research because he's going to be a doctor one day. I think he just likes killing them. He's horrible. He's as fat as the ticks Salena takes off Tommy-Tiger, but Ma always dishes up more food for him.

Each night we sit at the kitchen table, Papa, Faruk-Paruk, Salena and me. Ma eats standing up at the kitchen sink so it's easier for her to reach the pots on the stove and dish up second helpings for the men. Every night Papa tells me to stop wasting my food and to think of the children starving in India. I think of the children starving in India and wonder why they don't move.

I make hills out of the mushy white rice and turn the runny dhal into small muddy rivers. The overcooked vegetables are my trees and the fatty meat my castle walls. Faruk-Paruk eats everything on his plate, chewing with his mouth open, the food covering the knuckles of his right hand as he puts all four fingers deep inside his mouth. He always asks for and gets seconds. Salena finishes her tiny portion neatly and silently, the same way my cat Ginger washes his paws. She's so quiet, sometimes I forget she's there.

I want to eat Rice Krispies and bananas, like the picture on the cereal box. I want to hear them go "snap, crackle, pop". I'm hoping that one day when I open a new box those three little men on the front cover will climb out of the packet and I will train them to kill my brother, to slip inside his ear and smash his brain to bits with their snaps, crackles and pops!

Papa says we are not allowed to speak at the table during supper. But I can hear him breathing. I imagine the hairs in his nostrils (which he pulls out with the same tweezers Salena uses on the cats), blowing around as he breathes. Breathe out and they move forward towards the daylight. Breathe in and they are sucked back towards his brain.

Papa's a big man. I've watched him at weddings, talking to other men. Next to them he looks like the giant from *Jack and the Beanstalk*. Just yesterday he smacked Salena's face, and his palm and the hairy red knuckles on his hand covered her whole head! Papa's skin is usually very white, like a real white man's, but when he's angry he turns as red as Ma's sister Polla-the-Prune's lipstick, and greenish sweat drips from his black hair onto his skin. He uses green hair oil to make his hair flat. On the jar there's the face of a smiling man, but I've never seen Papa look like that.

Salena had black hair too, Ma says, when she was a baby. But now it's turned brown and shines red in the sunlight. Her hair's very straight and it's so long she can sit on it. My hair's black like Papa's and Ma's, but it's curly and always untidy. Ma calls it bushy hair. Ma's hair's invisible because it's covered by a scarf all the time.

Salena's white like Papa, but her skin's see-through like the plastic cover of a book. You can see the veins and blood underneath. I used to think Ma wished for Salena like Snow White's mother wished for her daughter. Then one day I overheard Ma tell Polla-the-Prune that there's only ten months between Salena and Faruk-Paruk because she had to have another baby quickly, as the first one was a girl. I don't like Polla-the-Prune.

Faruk-Paruk looks just like Papa. They could be identical twins, except Faruk's shorter and fatter – like he's been drinking from Alice's magic shrinking potion.

As usual, Faruk-Paruk's gobbling up his food. When he sees me looking, he opens his mouth wide to show me his tongue with half-eaten food on it and kicks me under the table. Pig. I hate him. Usually I don't do anything back. I'm scared Papa will smack me. But this time Papa sees what Faruk-Paruk has done. Without looking up or stopping his chewing, he reaches over with his left, clean hand and hits Faruk-Paruk on the head.

I lean back, in case there's a blow meant for me, but Papa's gone back to his plate of meat. He doesn't usually pick on Faruk-Paruk, because he's the favourite. I can't wait to start school next week so I can learn to read by myself. The school's not far from our house. Salena took me there yesterday to find out about my new uniform, and we met my teacher. I can't remember her name but her eyebrows are the colour of the sun, and she was wearing a long black dress. She said that she and the other nuns who are going to teach us are the brides of Christ.

Rukshana, a girl who's going to be in my class, said that maybe Christ is Muslim and that's why he has so many brides. Rukshana's father has two wives. I think Rukshana and me are going to be best friends.

. . . .

Rice Krispies with Bananas

Take a big soup bowl and pour in the Rice Krispies. Slice a banana
into the bowl, add 2 teaspoons of sugar and cover with cold milk.
You must eat this as soon as you've poured the milk,
or the Rice Krispies get too soft
and you can't hear them going snap, crackle, pop.

. . . .

Wedding Cake

FARUK-PARUK CALLS ME WORSIE LIPPE. I hate him. I wish he would die. He doesn't know, but I saw him bury his comics outside in the back yard. First, he put them in black rubbish bags and then he dug a hole to bury the bags because he doesn't want me to read them. Why would I? I hate silly Superman. I mean, he's got blue hair. How stupid is that? But I hate Faruk-Paruk more. When is he going to grow up? He's old now. Seventeen. If you say his name fast enough, with lots of rrrrrrs, it sounds like a frog croaking. Farrrrukparrruk. I think he is a frog, or a toad. Something slimy and cold.

I wish Salena wasn't getting married today, because my rose-pink dress is turning red as my nose drips drops of blood onto the lap of my skirt. I'm too scared to move. I don't want Ma to see that I've messed on my skirt. I don't want a hiding on Salena's wedding day.

I'm in our bedroom with Salena. She's sitting in front of the dressing-table mirror, her green eyes locked with her mirror-eyes. Aunty Polla keeps talking about how lucky Salena is to be marrying a lawyer. Ma says she's not sure if lawyers are as good as doctors.

Maybe I need a doctor. My lap is getting wetter. My blood is purple-red, like the bunch of roses Salena has to carry today when she walks up the aisle. Aunty Polla has finished making Salena's hair stand up as high as the wedding cake waiting in a white cardboard box on the floor for someone to take to the hall where the reception is going to be. I'm not going to eat the cake. I saw Tommy-Tiger stand with his back to the cake and lift his tail up high and let loose his yellow spray. I just hope the cake goes before the smell gets to Ma's Nancy Drew nose.

I think I'm choking, my throat feels thick. I push the little finger of my left hand into my right nostril. My madressa teacher said you can only clean your nose with your left hand because that is the hand the devil uses.

My finger finds a rubbery piece of blood. I pull it out and it plops onto my lap, a lump almost as big as my palm. At least I don't feel like choking anymore. Maybe Ma will feel sorry for me now. The blood is pouring from both my nostrils like the water in the tap I forgot to close the day I flooded the bathroom. That day I got a really good hiding.

Ma and Polla-the-Prune are fighting about Salena's hairstyle. Ma doesn't like what Aunty Polla has done. She wants Salena's hair flat and straight. Polla-the-Prune wants it high up in the air, so high that the planes flying over our house to the airport will smash into it.

I don't know what Salena wants. She's still staring at herself in the mirror. I try to move slightly so that maybe someone will notice me. Last week I had my first nosebleed. It happened at school. The teacher made me put my head back all the way on my neck so I could feel the blood drip into my throat. It tasted warm and salty like the spiced beef Ma cooks on Sunday mornings. Rukshana said she read that you should keep your head forward and pinch the bridge of your nose. I didn't know my nose was big enough to hold all this blood. Or is it coming from my brain? What if my brain leaks onto my dress and I become as stupid as Faruk-Paruk?

If only Salena would look at me, I'd feel better. Maybe now that she's getting married she'll forget about me. I wonder what will happen to me when Salena is no longer here to help me, to stop Ma shouting at me every time she has an argument with Papa.

There's a little blood-dam in my lap. It's going to soak through my skirt onto my white pantyhose. Ma calls them stockings. She bought me this pair with white roses on them all the way from Joburg, where she went to get her own dress for the wedding. Her dress is orange and gold.

Ma turns away from poking at Salena's head and looks at me. She curls back her lips, but before she can swear at me I burst into tears.

Then everyone is around me and they're pinching my nose so I have to open my mouth to breathe, and Ma's dragging off my dress and putting me into the bed Salena and I shared till last night. Last night, when she said, "I don't want to marry him, I don't want to marry him," over and over like a nursery rhyme, even though she was fast asleep.

I don't get a hiding. Someone calls for a doctor and someone else puts ice cubes wrapped in a cloth on my forehead. I lie back on the pillows and catch Salena's black-ringed eyes in the mirror. She shuts one eyelid. A wink. I wink back. But I can't do it properly yet, because both my eyes narrow at the same time, and then Salena smiles at me. "I love you forever," she whispers before they come in to take her away.

The doctor says I can't go to Salena's wedding. He says I should stay in bed. I don't mind. When they've all gone to the wedding and only me and the new maid Rosie are left behind, I climb into bed with my Nancy Drew book that I got from the library, and I'm glad I don't have to eat the wedding cake.

That night, my first night sleeping alone, I dream of hundreds of colourful eyes, opening and shutting and staring past me.

Ma Judas

I'M OLD, ALREADY NINE, AND IT'S EID and I keep forgetting to breathe, I'm so excited. Everything I'm wearing is new. I have on pink panties with a small bunch of red cherries embroidered on the right-hand side, a new white vest, fluffy white ankle socks, black patent-leather shoes with a T-bar and, best of all, a white dress that Ma finished sewing last night.

I was scared she wouldn't finish it in time. I lay awake listening to the sewing machine growling till my ears were too scared to listen anymore. The dress comes down to my knees, white satin and lace with puffy sleeves and a big satin bow at the back.

My black hair is pulled up into a ponytail tied so tight that my eyes look like Ginger's, and my hair swings from side to side with each bouncy step I take. After lunch we're going to visit Salena and her new baby, Muhammad.

Lunch is at the house of one of Papa's brother-cousins (not blood family, just same-Indian-village family). At least I think so, but in the car my father explains that the man we are visiting was on The Ship with him. I've heard about The Ship so often I feel like I was bombed by the Germans and left to drown in the icy ocean. During World War II, Papa and his mother, my daadi Bilqis, were travelling from India to Port Elizabeth when the enemy struck. They spent three days at sea, in lifeboats floating on the freezing water, before being rescued along with a few other survivors. I've been with Papa at weddings when he's met up with other survivors, and the women always cry and dab their eyes with the corners of their saris as they talk about not being eaten by sharks.

I wish Papa had been munched up by a shark. At least then I wouldn't have to listen to him breathing during supper, and if he were dead he wouldn't be able to shout at me all the time.

When we arrive in Rylands there are cars parked on both sides of the narrow road, and Papa squeezes his gold Mercedes between a bakkie and truck with extra care. He doesn't want this car, the love of his life, to be hurt. I push my book under the front passenger seat and make sure my door isn't locked in case I want to read in the car after lunch.

There are so many people in the house, it feels like a wedding. All the girls are wearing pretty, colourful dresses, and I love the women's gold and black beaded necklaces. I'm glad I nagged Ma into letting me wear her old dangly earrings and bracelet.

I greet everyone in the lounge and an old woman tells me to go to the back yard where the other children are going to watch the qurbani. I have no idea what she's talking about but I smile politely and do as she has ordered. The back yard is huge, filled with loquat trees and grapevines and six woolly sheep making baaing sounds. I have never seen sheep in real life. No one else seems surprised by them, and some children are even petting them. They smell funny. I'm not going to touch them.

Near the sheep there's a hole in the ground that someone has dug. Like a grave. Not that I've seen a grave, except in films, because girls aren't allowed to go to graveyards, or so Papa says. Then there's a man in white robes with a large knife in his hand. I think of the three blind mice. This must be a carving knife. And then there are more men and they are reciting from the Quran and I move forward and the man with the knife has his arm wound tightly around the sheep's head and, as I watch, something warm splashes on my satin dress. The smell slaps my face along with the baas of the other sheep. I run. Through the house, down the road, till I find the car and crawl into the back seat. In my mind I can still see the sheep moving even after its throat is slit, and I feel blood entering the top of my nose and the drops fall slow and heavy onto my lap, hiding the sheep's blood.

That night we drive home, and in the boot there is a bloody newspaper parcel filled with our portion of the sheep's body. The next day my mother will cook it into a curry and my food battle with her will begin. Until I learn to cook, I refuse to eat anything but Rice Krispies and cheese sandwiches. My mother tells everyone that I'm just going through a phase. She says it's because I'm spending too much time with Hindus like Rukshana – even though Ruks is Muslim like us (and some Hindus do eat meat, just not cows!). But Ma doesn't trust her because she's dark-skinned.

After that day I notice things I hadn't seen before. Cows in trucks turning into a long driveway in Maitland, near Polla-the-Prune's ugly house. When I ask my mother, she says they're going to the abattoir. I look up "abattoir" in the dictionary – it's a slaughterhouse where animals go to be killed.

I phone to ask Salena how the animals are killed in the abattoir, and she tells me. A sheep (or a goat) is trained to lead the others to their deaths. Usually this is a young ram, and when he has lived in the abattoir long enough and is used to the smell of blood, he leads the other sheep up the ramp into the slaughterhouse. The sheep follow, he escapes through a side gate, and they die. Later, when he gets older, they get a new Judas goat and the old one follows him to his death.

Salena says our mother and other women like her are Judas goats. They let girls follow them into the marriage-abattoir. I don't understand what she means, but she is sad when she says it. I wish I could make her happy.

....

Yummiest Cheese Sandwich

Take 3 pieces of your favourite cheese (mine's Gouda), 3 or 4 tomato slices, a few pieces of cucumber and some lettuce. Put them on buttered wholewheat bread and add lots of salt and pepper. Mmmmm!

....

Poor Skollie

For three Friday nights in a row, Ma's yellow Mazda has been broken into. It has to stand outside in the driveway because my father parks his gold Mercedes in the garage.

The first Friday they broke her passenger window and stole her radio. The second Friday they broke her driver's window and stole the replacement radio. The third week she left her car doors unlocked, but they still broke the window. Ma says they just like the sound of glass breaking.

I say "they", but Ma thinks it's just one skollie – she found only one set of footprints in the sand next to her car, near the cement driveway. She says they're the print of sandshoes. Everyone knows skollies wear sandshoes so no one can hear them prowling around at night.

My father is tired of the skollie, and Ma's swearing Big Bad Words every Saturday morning, so he's gone to the architect to start plans to build another garage. But Ma wants blood. I'm scared, but I'm glad it's the skollie's blood she wants and not mine. Poor Skollie.

That Friday afternoon, the fourth Friday afternoon since the start of the break-ins, Ma sends me to the cornershop to buy two bottles of cooldrink, but it's closed because of a death in the family. We drive to Grand Bazaars in Parow, the closest supermarket. She parks in the parking lot behind Voortrekker Road and gives me strict instructions. I must buy one litre of Coke and one litre of Fanta and nothing else. Not even my favourite caramel dessert with its bright-white creamy topping. She gives me a two-rand note, and off I go.

Ma stays behind in her yellow car, in her yellow safari suit, wearing big black sunglasses that leave only the tip of her pointy nose exposed. Ma wears a black hairpiece so she can have double-storey hair like the women in the movies and so that no one can notice her bald spot. She looks pretty. Usually she doesn't wear her scarf when we go to Grand Bazaars, so the white people won't know she's Muslim. But today she is wearing a big flowery scarf and only her fringe is exposed. I know she's in disguise, and her plans for Skollie have something to do with the cooldrinks. Poor Skollie.

We go home and Ma opens the Fanta and Coke and starts muttering. I realise she's making a potion for Skollie. Salena will love this! I am torn between wanting to watch Ma and the need to phone Salena, but I decide to watch. That way I'll have more to tell Salena.

First, Ma throws some of the green pellets she uses to kill snails into the grinder. She turns the pellets into a fine dusty powder that makes me sneeze three times in a row, and then adds equal amounts of the dust to both bottles. Then she adds Brooklax, the stuff she takes when she can't pooh. This she also grinds to a powder before she adds it to the bottles. She tells me to check the bottles to see if they have changed colour. (She needs spectacles, but she won't wear them. Salena says it's because she doesn't want to look old.) They haven't. She adds a bit of sugar to both bottles, which makes their gas bubbles rise, and then she closes the bottles tightly and puts them back in the Grand Bazaars packet.

After supper, Ma goes out in the dark and places the Grand Bazaars packet on the back seat of the car, so it looks as if someone has left them there by mistake. I ask her what will happen if the skollie gives the drinks to his children. She says that's his problem, not hers.

The next morning I'm up early and I rush outside to the car. I'm disappointed to see none of the windows are broken, but I investigate and find that the back door has not been closed properly. I open it, and the shopping packet is gone!

I run in to tell Ma. I am so excited, I can hardly eat. I imagine Skollie is in hospital, even dead! Ma says I'm not allowed to write about this in my News Diary at school on Monday. Now the wait begins.

The following Friday no one breaks into the car. Or the next. My mother, the skollie killer. And she didn't even know him. What could she do to me? I decide to stop drinking Coke at home.

Adopted

It's Thursday night, holy night, says Ma, and tells me to recite from the Quran. I say no. The words are meaningless old Arabic that I've memorised like a nursery rhyme. And at the age of eleven, I'm too old for nursery rhymes. I'm already an aunt to three children!

Ma says I am too big for my boots because of all the books I read. When I still refuse to say the words, Papa gets angry and smacks me. The yellow ring that he has recently taken to wearing on the pinkie of his left hand grazes my cheek and it begins to bleed. The sight of the blood seems to satisfy Papa. Then he tears up some comic books that are lying around the house. The funny part is that they aren't mine, they're Faruk-Paruk's, and the even funnier thing is that Papa can't read or write in English. At school, my teacher tells me I'm very clever. I can spell any word she gives me, even backwards.

S-D-R-A-W-K-C-A-B.

Faruk-Paruk screams at Papa when he gets home and they have a big fight. Later Faruk-Paruk gets me alone and tells me I am adopted. He says my real mother and father left me in a bin. I hope that's true! Faruk-Paruk says Ma took pity on me and my ugly lips and kept me. I wish she'd left me in the bin. Just to make sure, I ask Ma for my birth certificate, but she says she's lost it.

Now I know why Ma hates me. Why she always lets Faruk-Paruk lick the cake bowl and gives him seconds, when I'm only allowed one portion. It explains why I'm so dark and Salena's so fair. Ma, I mean my evil stepmother, is always comparing us. Telling me how white Salena is and how black I am. Ma says I should stay out of the sun or

I'll end up as dark as my Hindu friends. She caught me comparing our noses today. Mine is as flat as a pancake compared to hers. Obviously she cannot be my mother. But why do people say I look like Papa? What if Papa is my real father but he married a second wife and she died and he gave me to his first wife, Ma? No, that's not possible. Ma would never have allowed my father to marry anyone else, unlike Rukshana's mother.

A few days later I visit Rukshana at home. While we're eating the cake her mother made, I ask her if she thinks I could be adopted. Ruks says Ma is much too mean to ever look after another woman's child. She says I have to be her real daughter. She says Faruk-Paruk must be lying. I suppose she's right. Rukshana's father has two wives, and they live right next door to each other. He spends one night with Rukshana and her brothers and mother and the next night with his second wife and their children. They're neighbours, but Ruks says her mother won't let her play with her father's other children.

Rukshana says I should ask Salena. She should know. She was ten when I was born. But when I phone Salena the next day she can't understand me. Ever since the twins were born, a year after Muhammad, she always looks half-asleep. When I speak to her she doesn't seem to hear me and it's impossible to have a conversation on the phone because there's always a baby crying in the background.

After the cake we have to stay out in the garden because it is Tuesday and Rukshana's father has customers. They come to him to get rid of the jinn who have possessed them. I don't like the sweet smell of the incense he burns while he works. When we were younger Rukshana and I use to chase the incense smoke, pretending it was a ghost. He gets paid a fortune for removing the jinn and putting them in containers – jars, bottles and metal boxes. Rukshana says that's why he can afford two wives and so many children.

Once, Rukshana's father found us rubbing a jinn-jar, hoping that if we released it the jinn would grant our wishes. Her father explained that these jinn are made by Allah, from smokeless fire. They are not like the jinn in *Aladdin's Tale*, although they can fly around the world in the blink of an eye. They were created along with angels and people, and they can be good or bad and make their own choices. Sometimes a bad jinn slides into a person's body and starts to control them. It's Rukshana's dad's job to remove jinn from people and trap them so that they can't cause mischief.

Why would you choose to live in someone's body when you were free to fly? If I could fly, I would escape and try to find my real parents. Rukshana has just finished reading a book about an orphan boy called Oliver, who's just like me. She says I'm going to miss her when Ma puts me in the new high school. Rukshana's father wants her to stay on at the Catholic girls' school, so she won't get ideas about boys. Why are parents so stupid? Rukshana doesn't even like boys.

Cinderella's Wish

Once upon a time there was a little girl called Cinderella, who was treated very badly by her family. Her father had two wives, and whenever he went away with her mother he would leave Cinderella behind with his first wife and their two daughters. As soon as her parents left, the stepmother would hand Cinderella a uniform of rags to wear and give her a list of jobs to do in her father's cornershop.

Sometimes, when she was finished sweeping the shop, filling the paraffin bottles, packing the fridges with cooldrinks and washing out the drinking straws, her stepsisters would ask her to play with them. But they could not find a game to play that made them all happy. The older stepsister wanted to sit in front of the mirror and get the younger girls to paint her face with make-up. The younger stepsister wanted to catch butterflies and tear off their wings. Cinderella wanted to play school-school. Since they could never decide on one game, they soon stopped trying to play together or even talk.

One night Cinderella got into bed feeling fed-up. She was tired of her stepmother making her work in her father's shop and she hadn't seen her parents for months. As she tickled her cat Tommy-Tiger under his chin, she said to him, "I wish I had a different life!"

Suddenly a bright light filled the room and Cinderella watched as Tommy-Tiger jumped off the bed, stretched his furry muscles and turned into a woman, the same height as her, dressed in a loose silver burqa which left her emerald eyes showing.

"Tommy-Tiger, you're a woman! How could you keep a secret like that from me?" cried Cinderella.

"No, you silly child," said the voice behind the shiny material. "I belong to the jinn race. I've been watching over you for years. You have a very brave heart. I'm here to grant you a new life. You'll have new clothes, jewels, and of course a prince for a husband, and you'll bear him many fine sons. Let's begin. First, you'll need— What's wrong? Why the sad face?"

Cinderella looked into the jinn's green eyes.

"It's kind of you to give me a new life, but I don't want to get married, and definitely not to a man I've never met, even if he is a prince. My mother and stepmother are married, and they don't seem all that happy."

"So you don't want me to change your life?"

"Oh I do, please Tommy-Tiger! I want my wishes to come true. I wish," Cinderella looked down at her palms and then spoke in a small whisper, "to study."

"Well, Cinderella! That's the strangest wish I've heard in all the hundreds of years I've been granting wishes, but I'll do it."

Cinderella reached over and hugged the cloaked figure; it was like holding warm, perfumed air.

"Will you stay with me, Tommy-Tiger? You're the only creature in the whole world I love."

"Of course I will! I'm your guide forever, and I love you too. Now take a step back, child, and look at your surroundings."

Cinderella let go of the jinn and her mouth dropped open. Her bedroom had vanished, and they were standing in the middle of a gigantic library filled with books. Cinderella wept for joy.

Family Lice

It's a Wednesday morning in the December holidays, and Ma is cutting my hair on the front stoep. I want to go to a proper hairdresser but Ma says my hair is kroes, and she's not wasting money on it. The sun burns down on my scalp, but she gives me a piece of Lunch Bar to munch on, and soon I forget what she's doing. I can smell the red carnations from where they are planted near the garden gate – they're my favourite flower. They smell of cinnamon.

I'm going to be in Standard Five next year. I hope my new teacher's as nice as this year's. Last week Ruks and I met at Elsies River Library, and we got two copies of *Jane Eyre*, which we're reading together. Jane's an orphan girl (I love stories about orphans) with a wicked aunty who reminds me of Polla-the-Prune.

Ma lifts the weight of my hair up from the nape of my neck with her left hand. The right one holds a silver pair of sewing scissors. With the hair lifted I can feel dozens of little feet on the nape of my neck, sending tingles up into my scalp. The scissors open and close in her hand, like a baby's mouth searching for food. I hear the crunch as the scissor snip snip snips through my hair, munching, swallowing long threads of me, leaving my neck naked and cold and light. Free.

Ma turns me to face her and smiles at me and it feels like the static shock I got once when I was pushing the trolley in Grand Bazaars. I can't remember when last Ma has smiled at me or anyone else. She looks different when she smiles. She usually looks angry and serious, with the skin above her black eyebrows in wavy lines. She tells me I look much brighter now, as if I've had a bath. I remind her that I'm not a baby anymore, that I've stopped bathing and only take showers. She shakes her head at me and looks sad again. She says she can't believe I'm such a big girl. It seems like just the other day she told my father she was pregnant with me. Her eyes go hard again for a moment, and she stops smiling and turns me away from her.

Around the chair my hair floats on the ground in a dark puddle, still wet with my summer sweat, still moving with my lice. I watch the aimless journey of one louse, then another, then another, until there are dozens of them on this, their eviction march. I know how they feel. They walk up and down the strands, hunting for my missing scalp. They look confused. I lie down with my chin on the floor, so that I am on eye level with the lice, and then I put my thumbnail above one, bearing my nail down until I hear a soft click. My thumbnail is red with my own blood and bits of brown lice legs. Half the body is see-through, the other still holds onto my blood.

Ma comes back and sweeps my hair, a living, coiling mass, into the dustpan, and then goes off to bury it. I look in the mirror and a new face stares back at me. I don't know who that girl is. But I know she is alone without her lice friends, and when I begin to cry Ma says not to worry, my hair will grow again. But I am not crying for my hair. I am crying for my homeless lice. Ma gives me a cup of masala tea.

Sometimes I don't think Ma's really a wicked stepmother. She's definitely not as bad as Polla-the-Prune. Earlier today The Prune phoned to speak to Ma, and I shouted something like, "Your sister's on the phone." When Ma took the phone, Polla told her I was the rudest child she's ever known. Now Polla's told their cousin that I must be punished. I'm not allowed to be bridesmaid for the son or daughter who's getting married next month. I'm so happy! She doesn't know she's done me a favour. I was dreading the thought of having to wear something purple and balloon-like, and putting make-up on my face. Rukshana says that when you're a bridesmaid all the ugly boys and their uglier mothers watch you on the stage and decide if you're good enough to marry. Polla-the-Prune thinks I won't be able to get a husband if I'm not a bridesmaid. She's an idiot.

That afternoon, when Ma sends Ruks and me to the post office to mail money to Polla (she's poor because her husband left her for a coloured woman) I change the address on the envelope to the SPCA's. Ma will think the post office stole her money, but Ruks says at least I'll know a more deserving bitch got the money. If my Ma heard me say something like that she'd tell me I'm going to the Shaytan – never mind that *she* swears all the time.

....

Soothing Masala Tea

3 cups water

4 teabags

3–4 elachi pods, crushed

3 cloves

1 cinnamon stick

chunk of fresh ginger

9 tsp sugar (or to taste)

milk to taste

In a medium pot, add 3 cups of water, the tea bags and the coarsely ground spices. A mortar and pestle is best for grinding the spices. You should also add the sugar now, at least 9 teaspoons, but you can make it sweeter if you want.

When the water's boiled, lower the heat and let it simmer for a few minutes so that you can smell the tea even if you're in another room. Then add the milk until the tea is the colour of caramel toffee. It shouldn't be too white and milky. This is a good time to look for biscuits, something plain, like shortbread.

When you think the tea is ready, take it off the stove and use a tea strainer as you pour it into your cup. The tea strainer makes sure you get all the flavours with none of the yucky bits (if you bite on a piece of elachi, it's disgusting!).

Ma always used to give me masala tea when I got wet in the rain walking home from school. It warmed me up every time. Salena told me that our daadi said if you're ever scared you should make masala tea and recite Surahs Falaq and Naas over your cup before you drink it, to protect you from harm, envy, black magic and, of course, the evils of the Shaytan.

. . . .

The Thirteenth Floor

WHEN MA ANSWERS THE PHONE SHE BECOMES HYSTERICAL. She screams, she cries and then she smacks me. I have no idea why till she babbles crazily that Papa is in hospital. She phones Salena and then forces me into the car with her.

When we get to Groote Schuur, my father is hooked up to tubes and bossy beeping machines and he can't speak because there is an oxygen mask over his face. His body is black and navy blue like a rotten banana from all the holes left in him by the tubes sprouting out of his skin. You can see the blue-green veins just underneath his milky-white skin carrying his blood.

I have been left alone in the hospital room with him, to guard him like a Rottweiler, while Ma talks to the doctors. I don't want to be this close to my father. He stares at me with his cow-brown eyes and makes cutting gestures with the fingers of his left hand. I understand: he wants me to bring him scissors, to cut off the tubes, and I nod in pretend agreement. I am thirteen years old, and the cleverest in my class, but which person in white is going to give me scissors?

I go into the passage and my mother has her back to me and the doctor is saying, "Nothing to do, morphine," and Ma is nodding and agreeing, and she seems sad, but when she turns towards me there is a wild gleam in her eye, like I've seen in Ginger's eyes when he's fighting for the affections of a she-cat in heat. Then she sees me watching and the shutters come down over her slit-eyes.

I go off to play in the cavernous lifts of the hospital, imagining all the bodies that have been in them, living and dead, ghosts and people.

I have a newfound fascination with lifts, since Papa's accident. He went into town to fetch something from an office in Strand Street, and when he was leaving, got into the lift. The doors were open because they were doing maintenance, and someone had forgotten to put up the warning signs. Papa fell thirteen floors. One for every year of my life. Ironic, as my English teacher would say.

The hospital lift takes me down and up and down again, and I wander through the emergency section. No one stops my explorations. In one room I see nurses and doctors scurrying around frantically, while someone applies what looks like jumper cables to a body on a gurney.

Back in Papa's room, his cousin-brothers are sitting at his deathbed reciting from the Quran in serious voices. Salena is there with her husband, Mr Boring-Lawyer, and her three boys. The twins, dreamy Makeen and noisy Raqim, are identical boy-dolls, and Muhammad is really clever. I'm teaching him to read. Sadly, Faruk-Paruk is there too, reading Papa's medical information. The show-off. He's even worse now that he's emigrating to Australia with his irritating wife, who pinches my cheeks all the time. He's already putting on a fake Australian accent. He makes me sick. He probably makes lots of people sick, so it's a good thing he's going to be a doctor soon.

I have to get away from the keening prayers and the sharp antiseptic smells, so I escape with Muhammad, and together we play in the lifts – up and down, down and up. And I think of my father.

Then Faruk-Paruk finds us, and says I have to say goodbye to Papa. When we get back to the room, he's dead. Dead but not gone, and they tell me to kiss him. What? There is a voice laughing in my head. I've never kissed him before. He's never touched me, unless you count the odd smack. Now I have to touch my lips to his face. They must be crazy. I lean forward, my long curly hair hiding my face, acting as a curtain between my father and the deathbed audience. I make a loud dramatic smacking noise before turning away.

He's dead, but things are just beginning. A cousin-brother has brought his bakkie, and they take the body downstairs. Papa is wrapped in a hospital sheet but the staff won't let their sheet leave the hospital. Another cousin-brother comes to the rescue with a blanket from the boot of his car, and they wrap him in that, but it is too short and his grey-white veined feet stick out.

They stuff him into the bakkie and speed off, and one by one the other cars drive away and I'm alone in the hospital parking lot. They've forgotten me. Maybe the funeral will be all over by the time they realise they've left me behind.

But then Salena and the boys are behind me, ushering me into her car. On the way to Cravenby she stops to buy the kids and me faloodas. She says we need the sugar because of the shock. As I slurp mine up it tastes like Sunlight soap because I can't get the smell of hospital out of my nose.

At home, someone has covered all the mirrors with sheets. I think they're scared my father will catch a glimpse of himself in the mirror and be trapped forever in the house. Or maybe my mother doesn't want to see the look of joy in her reflection. She's got to go on pretending to herself and everyone else, or what will people say?

The men are carrying cotton wool and buckets of water into the guest bedroom, where they're washing the body. The body who was my father. My Father Who Art in Heaven. I'm so glad that, because I am a girl, I'm not involved in the washing. Faruk-Paruk has to deal with that, precious son. I catch a glimpse of him wearing his serious "As a Med student I deal with dead people all the time" expression.

Mental note to self: do not be in the country when Ma dies. I don't want to help with the washing of her body. It's bad enough catching her when she's asleep, her mouth empty of teeth as her and Papa's dentures swim in a glass of water next to their bed.

When the men are done washing Papa, his body resembles an Egyptian mummy, wrapped in layers of white cloth. His face still shows, with cotton wool stuffed up his hairy nostrils and pushed deep in his ears. They roll him out on a stainless-steel gurney, to the dining room, where they sit around praying, their bodies rocking backwards and forwards in a hypnotic rhythm which I can't bear to watch. I will certainly never eat in this room again. In fact, I might develop an eating disorder.

I am the right age, according to the magazines Rukshana lends me.

I amble around the house trying to find a peaceful corner. Ma is handing out wads of money to her sister and, for once, The Prune's face is lit up, like a chandelier. Of course, she's probably plotting to overcharge my mother in some way for the food she says she will make. Another cousin-brother has brought in two huge gleaming pots. Salena's twins waste no time in jumping in, one to a pot. Mmmm, boy-curry.

The kitchen is filled with the smells of oil and garlic and onions frying for the akhni, and I feel ill. Food is cooking while my father lies in the dining room with cotton wool stuffed up his nose. Maybe they don't want him to smell the food.

I don't know what to do, where to go, and though I wander through the house avoiding my mother's "Wear a scarf, what will people say?" I still find my way back to the body. Papa is exerting a form of magnetic control over me. I have to make sure he really is dead.

I watch from a corner of the room, from the floor, and Tommy-Tiger finds my lap the perfect base from which to observe and spit hate at all the strangers in his house. He's become very antisocial now that he's about a hundred cat-years old.

Finally, curiosity makes him move forward to the table, to pad up to the body, to touch the face with an interested paw, to prod it gently. He waits for my father to react, and so do I, but nothing happens. The face remains still, the eyes do not open, the hand does not swipe the cat away, so I edge forward and pick up the confused feline, and my mother notices me and says to put on a scarf, but in the voice she uses in front of other people.

I find solace in my bedroom with the twins and Muhammad, and behind the locked door we watch their favourite video, *Charlotte's Web*, softly, so no one discovers our sacrilegious behaviour.

And even when the body is gone, it is not over.

The men come back from the graveyard, and they eat and drink and talk and talk and shout. This is not what I thought mourning would be like.

Days later there are still visitors arriving to offer their condolences to Ma. People who were at the funeral and people who weren't. They all expect food and tea and Coke and coffee.

Ma gets the death certificate with my father's name on it and it says "Never married", and she screams and screams and people explain that Islamic marriages are not legal, but she will not be calmed.

Afterwards, I go to school, and everyone looks at me funny and says sorry. I don't know why. I'm not sorry.

· ·

Easy Falooda Milkshake

1 cup cold water

2 tbsp sugar

2 tbsp rose syrup

1 tsp agar-agar powder

2 tbsp falooda seeds

½ cup boiled water

2 l full-cream milk

2 tbsp rose water

½ cup rose syrup (less or more depending on your preference)

½ tsp elachi powder

more sugar to taste

Boil the cup of water, sugar and two tablespoons rose syrup. When it begins to boil, add the agar-agar and stir until it thickens. Remove from heat, pour into a bowl and refrigerate until firm like jelly. Place the falooda seeds in the boiled water until they are swollen. Strain, and allow to cool.

Once the jelly has set, grate it roughly. Pour the milk into a jug, add the rose water, rose syrup, elachi powder and sugar to taste. Pour into individual glasses, add some grated jelly, a teaspoon of falooda seeds, and stir. You could add ice-cream if you need the sugar rush and chopped nuts if you want to pretend it's healthy. Not that falooda isn't good for you, especially this recipe, with agar-agar (made from algae) instead of gelatine, which comes from the bones and skins of animals. Yuck! Falooda is refreshing on a hot day, and it's full of calcium, especially if you add fresh cream.

. . . .

Nuns and Dwarves

Papa's been dead almost a year. The shop's been sold to a cousin-brother and Ma's bossier than ever now because she got the money from the sale of the shop and she's in charge of the capital Papa inherited from Daadi – riches that our grandfather left Daadi and which she grew through wise investments. At least that's what Salena tells me. Salena says if Papa had been in charge of the money, he'd have lost it on the horses long ago. That's why our daadi had it put in a trust fund. I didn't know Papa gambled.

Ma seems taller, or maybe it's that she walks with her back held straighter, like my new PE teacher is always trying to get us to do. I hate the new high school Ma's forced me to go to. I miss Rukshana and all our calm nun-teachers. My new teachers are stupid.

Today we had to do "free writing" in class. Of course it's not really free, because it gets marked and the dumb teacher gives us the topic. We had to describe our family. It was harder than I expected. Eventually I started describing Salena, because I thought she'd be the easiest. I wrote about how she spends most of her time cooking, cleaning and running around after her boys, even now that there are only two of them. I didn't write about how in the middle of all her work she never misses a chance to throw a glance at herself in the nearest mirror. She'll pause, suck in her narrow cheeks, arch her brows, puff out her skinny lips (nothing like mine!), smile politely at her reflection and then go on chasing after the boys. It's a weird habit.

Then I moved on to describing Ma and became completely stuck. What could I write about Ma? How when I was little, Ma would scrub me daily, during my hated bath, as though she was determined to wash away my dark skin and reveal my fair self? Or maybe I could describe Ma's convoluted classification system, which would rival the government's own labelling categories. For example, Rukshana has a rich father (+ + +), and she's skinny (+ + +), but dark, aka a darkie (– – –).

In the end I decided to write about Ma's food. It's funny: even her cooking has changed now that Papa's dead. Everything she makes seems to taste better, and she often cooks my favourites, like veggie breyani, and soji for dessert.

I couldn't decide if I should say anything about Papa. So I just wrote that he is dead. I'm sure that made the teacher feel awkward. I hope so.

Generally, the teachers at my school are an odd bunch. Another thing to thank the government for: divided education. There aren't enough Indian teachers in Cape Town because the Indian community here is small, so they import these cast-offs from Natal who pay back their college tuition by accepting jobs in the Cape. The interesting ones never stay long.

This year there was Miss Naidoo, who taught us English for three weeks. She was about six foot tall and really clever. But one day she just disappeared: she was there on a Tuesday, and on the Wednesday she was gone. Apparently she went to study in England. Then there was Mr Jeenah, her replacement, who taught us for a single week. He wore the same white shoes, cream pants and green shirt with a matching green tie for the duration of his stay, and he never once looked up from the book he read aloud in a whisper. I was riveted. The rest of the class seemed equally hypnotised: no one said a word during five periods of English. But the next Monday he too was gone.

There's been no one interesting since then, unless you count the revolting Mr Ramphalsingh, or Rumpelforeskin, as we call him, because of his diminutive height, childish temper and perverted ways. His favourite "punishment" is to run his hand down the backs of his female pupils and snap their bra straps. Even the boys in the class have grown out of this game. I tried to tell Ma about it once, but she wouldn't believe me. "At an Indian school? You must be imagining things. You need to stop reading all those books – they're giving you ougat ideas!"

Rukshana says I should make a voodoo doll of him and stick pins in it. I don't know how she knows this stuff. I wish I was still at the Catholic school – I'd rather deal with crazy nuns than be at the mercy of an evil dwarf.

Hide and Seek

YIPPEE! THE JUNE HOLIDAYS ARE HERE – three teacher-free weeks and two and a half years before I'm over and done with school. Oh bliss. Oh joy. Every time I tell Salena I'd love to leave school and get a nine-to-five job so I can be free to pursue the really important things in life (like eating lip-smacking food and reading till the early hours of the morning) she looks at me in horror. Like I've suggested we hack Ma to pieces and bury the chunks in the back garden with Tommy-Tiger and Ginger and those comics Faruk-Paruk used to stash in the ground like family skeletons. I'm glad that he and that annoying wife of his have finally run off to Australia.

I'm spending a few days with Salena and the boys because Zain is away on business. Of course I'd never sleep over if Zain were at home. He reminds me of a cross between Rumpelforeskin and a zombie. Last Eid, when Ma and I came over for lunch, his entire extended family was there, and he kept introducing me to his repulsive relatives as his second wife. Not even the vomiting noises I made put him off. He's disgusting.

The boys and I are playing hide and seek in the garden. They're supposed to be hiding, although I can clearly hear their whispers from where they're crouching behind the stump of the loquat tree. I can't understand why Salena had the tree chopped down – I used to love picking off the loquats, still warm from the sun, and popping them into my mouth. Like eating bread straight from the oven.

Raqim's black cat Peanut Butter and I are meant to be looking for the boys, or pretending to look, but we're both too lazy to get up from the swing. Actually Peanut's the real reason I can't get up. He's washing himself and it's rude to interrupt someone at their ablutions, especially if that someone is a cat. Cats are very particular about cleanliness, like Salena. One of my favourite stories from madressa is about the Prophet (Peace-be-upon-Him), a cat-lover, who, legend has it, cut away a piece of his clothing so that he would not have to disturb his cat, Muezza, who was napping on a part of his robe.

I'm conducting an experiment to see how clean cats are. Each time Peanut's done licking and sucking at one pristine paw and moved on to the next, I stroke the recently cleansed paw. Immediately he stops washing the one he's busy with and resumes licking the other. To get rid of my scent. I've seen Salena do a very similar thing: clean her bathroom, then shower, and then after that, clean her bathroom again. But I must stop torturing the cat. I can see two pairs of boy-eyes watching me. Ready or not, here I come!

Goodbye Rumpelforeskin

I CAN'T BELIEVE I'M ALREADY IN MATRIC. It's strange: I can remember the fluffy duck I used to play with when I was three and the first time I sat in a black-tyre swing, but I can't remember most of high school. It's as if I've been asleep and am waking up a few years later from a dull dream.

Aren't your teenage years supposed to be the best years of your life? I go from home to school to the library to home to school, and my greatest thrill is the weekly trip to the new shopping mall and its sweet-smelling shiny bookstore. I've discovered all sorts of women writers that I never knew existed, and who don't write about love affairs and marriage and children. Two of my classmates have dropped out of school because of unplanned pregnancies. Of course the new daddies don't have to leave school; they walk around with a swagger, like they've accomplished something.

I can't imagine wanting to touch a boy's body. Most of the boys in my school look like they bath on special occasions only. Some of them have brought dagga to school, but the thought of having to pay money to swallow smoke seems absurd to me. I'd rather spend my pocket money on books.

Getting up each morning for school is like watching the same horror movie over and over. Monday mornings are particularly gruesome, and they begin on Sunday afternoons as the weak Sunday light seeps away to make way for the new school week.

I can't wait to leave this school, especially to see the backs of certain teachers, like the hateful Mr Rumpelforeskin, who's become a whole lot worse this year. He's really losing it now: he stinks of alcohol all the time. And he's added a new dimension to his favourite punishment. Now, when he snaps our bras, he sticks his frosty parchment hands right down the inside of our school dresses, poking our skin with his bony knuckles as he hunts for the strap.

Why do we put up with it? We're almost grown up. But when he sidles closer, it's as though we've been turned to stone, immobile and without tongues. One day I tell him to fuck off, but he seems to find that a real turn on, and I get singled out two days in a row. At the end of the second lesson he tells the class we have to come in the next day for extra lessons, even though it is Saturday.

I oversleep that morning, so Ma drops me off and, because it is raining, she gives me one of Papa's old umbrellas to use when I walk home. I open the classroom door and look into the faces of my classmates, who are wearing identical expressions of horror and amusement.

Rumpelforeskin is standing at the head of the class as usual and, as usual, he is wearing his white lab coat, like the GP he will never be, but today it's open … and there's nothing underneath it! He is naked, displaying an anorexic abdomen and grinning like a demented gnome, exhibiting an obscene caterpillar of a penis swaying in a patch of pubic hair. He appears to be discussing the periodic table, and is oblivious to his audience.

I stand on the threshold of the classroom. It is a Saturday morning; I should be exploring the bookshop's shelves while Ma is at the shop next door buying expensive foundation several shades too light for her. Instead, here I am being scarred for life. This is not right. I walk out of the classroom, and when I get home I tell Ma the teacher was sick, which is the truth, if not the whole truth.

It seems my madressa teacher was right after all: it is important that people have honourable names with beautiful meanings. Mr R was simply living up to his sleazy nickname. I wonder if that means I'm going to be an astronaut.

On Monday I hear the rest of the tale. Rumpelforeskin went on teaching until one of the boys, whose house is across the road from school, got fed-up and went to fetch his father, who promptly called the principal and the cops. The next day we have a new teacher, Miss Roberts. I never see Rumpelforeskin again, but from time to time he visits my nightmares.

Makeovers

I'M AT VARSITY AND EVERYTHING AND NOTHING HAS CHANGED. I'm majoring in history because I have this vague idea that I'd like to become a teacher to compensate for all the rotten ones I had at school. Still, I'm not entirely satisfied with the idea of teaching as a career; I don't feel grown up enough to make any solid decision yet. Perhaps it would help if Ma showed an interest in my studies, but she's made it abundantly clear that she's prepared to fund my stay at varsity provided I make sure that somewhere along the line I bring home a doctor, or a dentist (I don't have the heart to tell her there's no dentistry faculty on this campus), or at the very least a pharmacist. Occasionally when she pisses me off I imagine bringing home a nice dark-haired Jewish doctor-to-be, who is deeply involved in the struggle and who likes darkies as Ma says.

Rukshana and I have met up again, although there's a certain distance between us now. The five years apart have changed us, and she's studying art and drama, which means she's on a different campus. We do meet up for English lectures, and we still have that ability to communicate without words, but the bond is not the same. She says it's because she's openly gay and I'm uncomfortable with that, but I don't think that's it. I tell her my hormones haven't kicked in yet and she rolls her eyes at me and offers to give me a biology lesson with a mirror, which makes us both cry with laughter, remembering how our madressa teacher once solemnly told a group of us twelve-year-old girls that if a husband looks at his wife's naked body during intercourse any child they conceived would be born blind.

Rukshana and another friend of hers, Maria, who is Greek and comes from a background as bubble-like as ours, see me as their pet project. They've forced me to free my hair, which for years I kept in a fish plait hanging down my back. Now I wear it loose, its abundant curls floating around me like a permanent cloak. I get stopped by white girls all the time to ask me where I had my perm done. I say Rylands, and they look back at me blankly.

Every Friday afternoon Ruks and Maria take me shopping in Claremont. I walk into the change room in my shapeless tracksuit pants and overlarge T-shirt and come out wearing slinky tops, tight little skirts and high heels that make walking impossible. They sing my praises and applaud. I tell them my rule is to never wear shoes you can't run in, and that goes for clothes too. We settle on shoes with flat heels and designer jeans with fitted shirts.

I admit to liking our forays into the make-up department more. They take me for facials, and my skin, of which Ma has always made me feel ashamed, glows. My eyebrows are plucked into perky curves, and I lose my moustache. I'm not an artist like Ruks, but I discover a knack for painting my face in the latest fashionable colours, and my lips, which I've been biting to make them smaller since Faruk-Paruk first told me they looked like sausages, become permanently stained in red.

When I go back to the house, silent except for Mr Humperdinck serenading Ma, there is no one to talk to about my week, or about the new me in the mirror. I don't know what Ma does during the week, but her weekend social life is restricted to our shopping-mall forays and Sunday-morning visits to Polla-the-Prune and lunch with Salena. The Prune never fails to mention that at my age she was married, and I never fail to ask her about her husband. Sometimes she pretends he's still living with her, but everyone knows about his new wife and their five children.

Every Sunday Salena cooks us a magnificent meal, including a vegetarian dish for me. I think she's on drugs: she wears the same serene expression of the Mona Lisa, and we hardly talk at all, unless it's about her sons.

In the late afternoon, while Zain naps, Ma and Salena drink tea together and the boys and I play in the garden. They catch frogs and spiders and put them in glass jars, and I pretend to eat them, before we let them free.

....

Potato Curry

2 tbsp oil

1 tsp cumin seeds

½ tsp mustard seeds

1 onion, finely chopped

1 tomato, finely chopped

½ tsp turmeric

1 tsp powdered dhania

½ tsp crushed garlic

½ tsp crushed ginger

1 green chilli, chopped

4 medium potatoes, peeled and cubed

salt to taste

1 cup water

finely chopped dhania leaves for garnish

Heat 1 tablespoon of oil in a pan and fry the cumin and mustard seeds. In a separate pot, fry the onions in the rest of the oil until golden brown, then add the tomato and cook until soft. If the mixture gets dry, you may need to add some water.

Add the fried cumin and mustard seeds plus the turmeric, powdered dhania, garlic, ginger, chopped chilli and salt. Mix in the cubed potatoes and water. Cook on a low heat until the potatoes are soft. Garnish with dhania leaves. A great dish for herbivores like me.

....

Promises, Promises

I wanted my golden ball. He said he could get it for me, if I rewarded him. I thought he would ask for a jar of flies that I could get a palace servant to collect for him. But Mr Froggy had aspirations. He wanted to eat from my golden plate, drink from my golden cup and sleep next to my golden limbs. It was horrific.

Daddy told me I'd made an oath, and I'd better honour it the way a true princess would (unlike Mom, who broke their marriage vows to run away with my governess).

But I knew what Daddy was thinking. If Mr Froggy could talk, he was probably a prince under a spell. Daddy imagined that if I helped free Mr Froggy from the spell, we would be obliged to marry. Daddy would be rid of me: no more memories of my mother.

No way was I travelling on a guilt trip of Daddy's plotting. A few hurriedly spoken words didn't constitute a verbal agreement, as far as I was concerned. Besides, there were no witnesses. I would not be bound to some slimy green creature that couldn't let an insect flutter by without unravelling its tongue to taste it. He revolted me. I didn't want to marry this amphibian; I didn't want his tadpoles swimming in my clean body every night. I thought of my cat Fluffy, overindulged, heavy with too much cream and her latest litter. She'd eat anything that didn't move.

That night, when Mr Froggy was asleep on my golden pillow, I sprinkled some of Fluffy's golden food pellets over his sleeping form and placed him on the pillow before her cat basket. One greedy gulp, a few chews, and bye-bye Mr Froggy. As painless a passing as I could arrange – I'm not cruel or vindictive. Just a bit self-centred.

Daddy woke us up as the sun threw its golden gaze into my palatial bedroom. I was exhausted. Fluffy had kept me up most of the night, meowing and coughing with indigestion. Daddy searched everywhere for Mr Froggy, to no avail. He frowned at me; I shrugged and began filing Fluffy's nails. He was suspicious, but of what could he accuse me?

Then it was my turn to remind Daddy of his agreement with me. The one he'd made on paper.

Next week Fluffy and I are off on a world tour. I've always dreamt of travelling – perhaps I'll even look up Mother, now that I'm of legal age and Daddy can't keep us apart any longer.

Macbeth

FINAL EXAMS ARE FINISHED. I'm the proud owner of a bachelor's degree, and I still have no idea what I want to do when I grow up. Rukshana has a job in an advertising agency. I'm a bit envious that she's earning a salary while I'm still Ma's dependant. I've decided not to study further for fear of living in books forever, so instead I've volunteered to teach English literature in a high-school enrichment programme in the Cape Flats, just for a year. It will help me decide if I want to go into teaching, and I'll be doing something useful for a change.

Ma's pissed off because I brought home a degree without a doctor-husband attached to it. She keeps muttering about the girls in our extended family who are as old as I am and have babies already, blah blah blah. She's not keen on my volunteer work because I'm unlikely to meet her dream-doctor in a township, but she's bought me a car and is paying for driving lessons. I've tried to convince Salena to join me in driving lessons; but she says her husband wouldn't want her to drive.

My job is simple enough: teach *Macbeth* to five classes of Standard Eights, in one-hour slots. Basically the same lesson five times a day to five different classes – but it's not as dull as it sounds.

Of course it helps that *Macbeth* is filled with murder and witches and blood that won't wash out, and the classes love it when I read them fairytales involving witches; the gorier the better.

One day during the June holidays I'm driving in the city on my way to visit Ruks at her work, and I hear a pedestrian screaming at me through the slow rain, "Macbeth, Macbeth", and it's one of my students. Fame at last.

Growing Up

I'M MOODY AND MISERABLE. Teaching is over for the year. Although it's only October, it's time for examinations, and the real teachers have taken over. I've loved *Macbeth*, but I've decided I don't want to make teaching my career. I'm restless, with an energy that has no outlet. Then I get a letter from Papa's sister in England. Aunty Anjum and her family moved there after they were kicked out of Kenya. Her correspondence has always been erratic, but somehow this letter seems like an answer to an unspoken prayer.

I practise the words for days, then mention to Ma as casually as possible, "Why don't I visit Papa's sister for a few months?" Ma frowns and says she'll think about it. I'm surprised I don't get her barely-there raised eyebrows, which she never needs to pluck. I know what she's thinking: the girl can't find a doctor-husband in Cape Town, maybe she'll meet a nice Indian boy in London. She calls up Aunty Anjum and they plot together.

I apply for a passport with some truly horrific photographs. Ma takes me shopping for winter clothes: thermal undies and socks, a new jacket. I feel like I'm five years old. Afterwards we drink coffee together and she tells me she might sell the house now that I'm gone, get something smaller. Has she realised I don't plan on coming back? Is she giving me permission to leave her forever? Is Ma growing up?

That December she sees me off at the airport, reminding me to be a good girl and not to bring shame on the family. Translation: Don't have sex, and if you do, don't get pregnant. Muslim mothers protect the hymen with the same energy conservationists use to protect endangered species. She reminds me to honour her; she tells me that according to the Quran, my heaven lies under her feet. I smile and nod agreeably, like I'm Salena. I'm afraid she may change her mind and hold on to my ticket. She touches my curls, tells me I can still have my hair straightened, even in London. Then she pats my cheek and says that at least I won't see the sun for a while.

From the plane window I can see the land growing smaller, until it is beyond my recognition. I'm excited to be leaving, and only wish Salena were coming with me.

The Ties That Bind

I haven't washed my hair in years. It stinks. I have split-ends that reach from the bottom of the tower all the way up to my waist. As for blow-drying it straight? Impossible without an army of hairdressers. It's because of her that it's in such a state – the spiteful bitch-witch. She placed me under this enchantment, gave me this ludicrously long hair. (Of course it's not naturally long – hair grows about a centimetre a month. Do the maths. How old do you think I am?) The colour? No, it's not my own, either. I used to be dark-haired, but she preferred this hue. How do the Grimms describe it? "Spun-gold". Spun-gold, my arse. She gave me this length, this colour, but she never thought of the maintenance! And now she's so old, she's forgotten her own spells. Bitch. Witch.

I beg her. I say, "I'll listen to all your ramblings, if only you'll cut it!"
But she says, "No, if it's gone, how will I get up here?"
I tell her, "Lady, you're a witch, fly up on your bloody broomstick!"
But she says, "I can't. I forgot where I parked it."
My bitch-witch. Stupid as my father, dumb as my mother. Both selfish and into instant gratification. Never thinking about me, stuck in the middle of a forest with a hag. Exchanged me for a bit of plant. It's no wonder I have self-worth issues.

So when he arrives, nervous, like a cat on crack, what can I do? He charms me, because I can't compare him to any other man. I don't know any men.

He says, "Your hair just gets in our way, let's chop it off."
I say, "Bitch-witch says men find long hair sexy."
He says, "Maybe, but not me, and not this long."
I ask him if he thinks I'm beautiful.

"Yeah, you're gorgeous, but I didn't fall in love with you because of your face. I couldn't see your face where you stood, way up in the clouds, your features obscured by your blonde tresses. It was your voice, it was your maudlin song; you vocalised my sorrows, my despair at being a prince in this dark land of hard-working heroines, wicked wolves, abusive parents, gold-grabbing kings and murderous tots.

"Your singing is sublime," he says. "We'll get you a record deal when I get you out of here."

He cuts my hair, as efficiently as any skilled barber. My nape is naked, and I am free of vermin and other hangers-on. He says, "Let's leave this place," and I say, "How?" He says, "Let's indulge in the power of positive thinking, or a spell: you must have learnt a thing or two from the witch?"

And I have. We clasp hands, we picture a white light around ourselves, we take deep cleansing breaths as the tower crumbles around us, and I am on terra firma again, free for the first time.

He says, "Let's go." And I say, "Listen, I know it's traditional for the heroine to marry her rescuer, but I can't marry you. You're the first man I've seen. I need to do some sexual experimenting first."

And he says, "Okay, I'll wait. And if you don't choose me, at least we'll make music together."

I sit on the front of his horse, my dress pulled up, my thighs spread on its furry, warm brown body, the back of my sparkling head resting against the prince's beating chest. My bitch-witch walks by. She doesn't even glance at us: she still can't see me.

He says, "Should I kill her with my sword?"

I say, "Nah, she's already dead to me."

New Beginnings

I'M IN LOVE WITH LONDON BOOKSHOPS AND THE SPEED of the Underground, and I think of the joy the clothes and shoes would bring to Ruks and Maria.

I'm so happy staying with Aunty Anjum. She dresses in jewel-coloured saris, like Salena told me our daadi used to wear and, like her mother, she also loves telling stories. Aunty Anjum has heaps of children and grandchildren – I can't remember all the cousins' names – and they all live together in a huge house on the outskirts of London, like one Big Happy Family. Aunty Anjum never got to see her mother again after they married her off at fifteen (to her first cousin – she didn't even have to change her surname) and our daadi came to South Africa. She looks sad talking about her mother. I try to sympathise. But I can't imagine longing for Ma.

I love Aunty Anjum's cooking, especially her moong dhal curry with rotis. It warms me up better than the central heating. While I'm scoffing her food she tells me stories, some about Papa. Apparently, back in India, my grandfather used to thrash my father and leave him hanging from a tree overnight. Well, that explains a lot – too late. She talks about people long dead as though we were all friends together, and sometimes she lapses into Urdu, forgetting I don't have a clue what she's talking about.

Aunty Anjum does her chores with one hand, the other holding her tasbih, praying silently. In the darkness of the morning I hear her reciting her prayers and it fills me with peace. Sometimes I watch her from the window of the attic, which is my bedroom, as she rakes leaves in the garden, still wearing the incongruous sari, her only concession to the freezing weather a minute pearly-pink cardigan.

Unlike Aunty Anjum, my cousins, at least the unmarried ones my age, are more English than Muslim. (Ma wouldn't be impressed with their love of pub-culture.) They don't seem to carry a sense of guilt about being Muslim at home in front of their mother and being like the rest of society when they're at school or at work. I suppose it's not that different from the schizophrenic life I led with Ma.

Then I find him, or, as he says, he finds me, although neither of us was lost, only a little misdirected. He's called Jim, and he lives a street away from Aunty Anjum, and the first time I see him I'm walking home from the café and he's putting up lost-and-found posters for the ugliest cat I've ever seen. It's black, with one eye and one and a half ears. He says it's not really his cat: it belonged to his dead mother. I like the idea of a dead mother, but what I like even more is the way he looks down into my eyes, and the soles of my feet respond by burning. We have a conversation about cats, but I don't think I'm making much sense because my brain is trying to regulate my heartbeat and blood pressure, and my hormones have gone mad.

Days later the cat is still missing, and I can't get through the day without hearing Jimmy's voice. Part of me knows I am behaving like a stupid girl, and that part whispers cynical things in my ear, but the stupid-girl part muffles the whispers with loud sighs. I don't feel cold any longer, my skin is burning up, and Aunty Anjum suggests a trip to the local GP because I look feverish and I keep putting the sugar in the fridge. I mumble something about the library and leave the house to meet Jimmy's train.

It takes me a while to understand what he does, because every time he talks I focus on his lips: they're pale pink, a bit like the lipstick Ma wears to weddings, but without the frosty sparkle, and the top lip's a little longer than the bottom. Eventually I understand that his business has something to do with hotels and laundering linen. I've managed to listen long enough to know he's an orphan (yippee!), twice over, in fact. Adopted when he was two from an orphanage in Guernsey and brought over to London by a wealthy middle-aged couple, who both died in a car accident a few years before we met. It's the dead father's business that Jimmy manages, but he says it can run itself. His passion is technology, and as a hobby he's restructuring his friends' businesses through the more efficient use of computers.

He's nine years and two weeks older than I am, and he's had three serious relationships. Ma would like the fact that he's pale and straight-haired. My favourite thing about him are his eyes. They're the same shade as the milky chocolate that keeps appearing on Aunty Anjum's doorstep, wrapped in silvery layers of paper.

Our first kiss is polite and strained and a letdown after all my fantasising, but when I finally manage to block out Ma's voice lecturing me about hymens, I'm happy.

. . . .

Aunty Anjum's Moong Dhal Curry

1 cup moong dhal

¼ cup water

½ tsp turmeric

1 tsp salt

2 tsp oil

1 tsp mustard seeds

1 tsp cumin

4 curry leaves

4 green chillies

2 pods garlic, cut into small pieces

1 tsp ginger

½ onion, chopped into small pieces

1 ripe tomato, cut into small pieces

dhania for garnish

Wash and soak the moong dhal overnight, or if it's a spur of the moment decision, place it in water in a microwave-safe dish and cook on high for 10 minutes. Place the dhal in a pot, cover with water, add turmeric and salt, and boil until soft.

In a pan, add the oil, mustard seeds, cumin, curry leaves, green chillies, garlic and ginger, and sauté them for a minute. Add the onion and fry until brown. Add the tomato and cook until soft. Now add the moong dhal mixture. Cover the pan and cook, for about 10 to 15 minutes.

You can garnish with fresh dhania leaves if you like. Guaranteed to take the chill off your bones, and perhaps invite love into your heart.

· ·

Travelling

WE'RE ON THE LONDON UNDERGROUND. I'm holding Jimmy's hand and the train is coming in two minutes, and the other commuters are complaining about the wait. Are they crazy? I remember my endless train journeys while studying at UCT. Ma would drop me off at campus in the mornings but I'd travel home by train. First there was the walk to Rondebosch station, then the journey from Rondebosch to Salt River and the endless wait in the middle of the day for a connecting train to Parow (until I learnt to spend my afternoons in the library). These Londoners are spoilt rotten.

Generally, I prefer trains to buses. I can read on trains and planes and even ferries, but buses are impossible; all that stopping and starting makes me nauseous.

When I was little, I would trundle upstairs to sit at the top of the bus, or at the back, if it was a single-decker. Sometimes Salena would sit in the front, at my urging, just for the sake of being naughty.

I recall one bus trip in particular. We boarded in Parow, and I begged Salena to sit in the front, right under the nose of the white conductor. I remember feeling excited, clutching a plastic bag filled with some of Salena's sugar biscuits for the trip. We were travelling to Mowbray – I can't remember why. And then, just past Elsies River, the bus stopped, and the conductor got off and was replaced by another, calling out, "Tickets, please."

My sister was the third passenger from the front. I was right at the back, against the window. She turned around and looked at me, her face filled with owl's eyes. I realised that I had the bus tickets in my pocket. I had insisted on buying and keeping our tickets. The conductor was still chatting to the man in the front seat, but any second he would be upon my sister.

How would she explain that a non-white child was carrying her ticket? I wished the bus would have an accident. Anything to make the ticket collector stop his journey to my sister. I clutched both tickets in my slippery-with-sweat hand.

Then an angel appeared. Right there on the bus, sans wings, but wearing a huge black doek. She took the ticket from me, and as my sister looked up helplessly into the white face of the ticket collector, she called out, "Here Miss Sarah, I have your ticket," pretending to be my sister's maid, and Salena came to the rear to fetch it, her eyes speaking her thanks. And when he was gone and had clicked my ticket too, I turned to the knowing gaze of the woman. "You children play dangerous games, just like my Sammy, and what did that get him? A bullet in his back." Tears came to her eyes. She took out a fluffy white handkerchief and wiped them. "Don't do it again, my girl, you can get your sister into a lot of trouble."

My voice squeaked out, "How did you know?"

"Ag, my girl, anyone with half a brain can see you're family. You look the same. Okay, this is my stop, and now you be a good girl, alright?"

I nodded. She smiled at me and lumbered off.

The woman had left me with a puzzling problem. I'd grown up knowing I was dark and therefore ugly. Compared to Salena, I was a brown gnome. How could this stranger have seen a resemblance? But she had.

In another hemisphere, the train arrives, and people push between Jimmy and me and we're separated, and I'm in the train but he's not and, "Mind the gap," says the robotic voice, and I stare at Jimmy through the glass and he mouths, "Get off at the next station and wait," and I nod. But I'm so afraid, my mouth is bitter, my armpits are tingling, and I think, "He won't come," but I get off and wait, and then he's there, and I cling to him as though we've been separated for years, and he laughs. He thinks I'm play-acting, and I smile too and giggle, and say, "They're tears of laughter," and I know I can't leave. I love him.

He's suggested, a bit too casually, that we get married. I think he's as afraid of rejection as I am of love. When I'm with him, we make perfect sense. When I'm not with him, I remember he's a white man. Jimmy says I'm nuts; it's just about him and me and our future together. I wish it were that simple.

Bear Hugs

GOD, I HATE THIS BLOODY WEATHER; IT'S NOT NATURAL. And I'm tired of studying. I'm doing my honours in English through Unisa, and finding it quite a challenge juggling coursework, a new job (even if it is only a part-time teaching position) and a husband!

I can't believe that I waved goodbye to Ma a mere two years ago, and I'm already a synthetic Salena. Well, not quite. Salena doesn't have to work or study. And at least we have a cleaner who comes in twice a week. Tilly worked for Jimmy's parents for ten years before they died, and is a bizarre source of information about the human body, on topics that range from in-grown toenails to premature balding in women. She wanted to be a nurse but dropped out after a term because "our Jenna was in the oven".

Tilly loves paging through our wedding album. Ma couldn't come for the wedding: she'd had an operation on her varicose veins. I never knew she had varicose veins – I don't think I've ever seen Ma's legs. She sent Aunty the money for the ceremony and gave me a set of jewellery that Papa had bought her when they got married. Salena, her two boys and Rukshana came for the wedding, or rather weddings. Aunty arranged the nikah – red sari, orange hands, dripping borrowed-gold, food and people everywhere – and Jimmy organised the legal ceremony.

Jimmy loves the idea that now he belongs to a huge family. The cousins are seduced by his endless chatting and his questions and his interest in learning more about every person he meets. I think he might even talk his way into Ma's heart if she can forgive him for not being a doctor.

Sometimes I wake up during the night and find Jimmy's arms and legs wrapped around my body and I'm convinced he's trying to kill me with his love. I've explained to him that while I shared a bed with Salena when I was little, as an adult I've only ever slept with a cat, and I like some space to breathe. Still, night after night I wake up clutched to his hairless chest, like I'm a human teddy bear. He's terribly cheerful every morning, bringing me the bitter coffee he's taught me to love while I pretend to be asleep, and many an evening he comes home with a gift. A book of love poems, a Russian doll in the shape of a cat, Belgian chocolates. I don't have the heart to tell him that I hate love poems, the nesting doll makes me think of coffins, and I no longer have a sweet tooth now that I'm on the pill.

But one weekend he goes away on a business trip, and I can hardly wait until bedtime to stretch out luxuriously in the centre of the bed, relishing having it all to myself. Only I cannot sleep, and I find myself longing for his overheated presence.

Teacher's Pests

Two years later I am still working as a teacher's assistant at a primary school ten minutes' brisk walk from home. I have to clean up after the kids (seven-year-olds), pack away books, wash paint brushes, straighten chairs and desks. The kids seem to vomit a lot: I believe it has something to do with eating too much chips and eggs fried in lard. I master the art of cleaning up vomit in three swift moves of a cloth while holding my breath to prevent the addition of my own undigested meal to the splodges on the floor.

They have no interest in the fairytales I try to read them. They ask me why Rapunzel didn't call the coppers. Did Cinderella at least get pocket money for all the work she did? Could I get them the video next time? I make them run around the classroom whenever I am left alone in charge of them. It keeps them quiet for a few minutes. One of the kids has an asthma attack during an indoor jog and the parents complain, so they move me to an older group.

I prefer the eleven-year-olds. They've been in school since they were five but some of them have managed to avoid learning to read and write, which is an impressive feat of subterfuge after more than six years. I am assigned to teach two boys and a girl how to decode the mysteries of the alphabet, and at the end of the first week I believe that I would have a better chance of succeeding in this task with a cat.

I can't teach them, but they teach me a great deal. About sex. Jimmy is impressed with my new knowledge. Education does broaden your horizons. I also learn to swear with true conviction. Jimmy is less impressed by this.

Finally we have a breakthrough when I walk into the girls' toilets and come across several variations of the word "fuck" written on the back of a cubicle door, all bizarrely misspelt. When I return to my pupils, I ask them to brainstorm all the swear words they can think of and all the sex positions they can name. I write these down on three pieces of paper, one for each child, in big block letters. We begin to learn the alphabet based on words that would make Jimmy cringe.

Before long, my little group can read and write their favourite words. I am delirious with pride; it's as satisfying as teaching *Macbeth*. We move on to words in their syllabus. Soon they can read at the level of eight-year-olds. The class teacher, Mrs Rutherford, an ancient thirty-five-year old with a permanent tic in her left cheek, is impressed with the improvement and asks me about my methods. I am vague and dismissive. They give me another group and a small increase.

The following December they offer to send me on a crash course in teaching, but by then I have had enough of teaching, forever. Besides which, Jimmy has sold the family business for a huge profit and has embarked on a new computer venture involving the Internet. He's suggested we move to the US for a while, says it's better for his business, and I say, "Let's go to Florida," because I'm reading a novel set in Miami and the characters are always sweating, even in winter. Jimmy says Florida's not the ideal American city for the business, but I tell him he can travel. I'm beginning to think that a long-distance relationship can only enhance one's marriage – all those delectable reunions.

Lessons

We had to leave; she wouldn't stop teaching us things. First it was potty-training, then bathing daily, then table manners. She made us chew a hundred times before swallowing; my middle sister couldn't even count past seven. Next we had to ask for the slop politely instead of grunting or swearing, as my littlest sister was fond of doing. She forced forks into our trotters and we were only allowed to eat what we could get on to the fork. We began to lose weight: we were starving!

She told us we should keep ourselves as clean and pretty as Cinderella. I know my limitations: I'm a pig, and I will never be beautiful. She told us we should be like Beauty with her head in a book all the time. She forced us to learn to read and write. I studied, and I coped, but it was difficult for my siblings, and I knew I had to take charge before things got worse for them. What was wrong with our mother? Why did she so care about what the other creatures thought of us?

I packed up our possessions, mostly hand-me-downs, and my sisters trotted off after me. She'd left us no choice. We travelled far and wide, foraging for food in the forest or begging at castle doors. At night we slept in fields, my sisters piling their bodies on top of mine, making it impossible for me to breathe freely. There were men with straw and sticks who agreed to build us houses for free, but we were reluctant to accept their offers: they seemed too good to be true.

Then one day we saw a sign in the window of a brick building. HELP WANTED. ENQUIRE WITHIN. He had heavy dark fur, and yellow eyes as hard as pebbles.

My baby sister asked, "Don't you eat pigs?"

"No," he said, "I'm Muslim."

He said that provided we could cook and keep the business clean, he would be happy to employ us all. We could live in one of the storerooms out back. We said we'd accept on a trial basis, and he agreed.

He was often away (he never told us what he did), but the business flourished under our care. My middle sister cooked, my baby sister served the customers, and I looked after the books. Whenever he returned, he would praise our management skills. After a few years he gave us one of the restaurants in his new franchise and helped us to buy a home, where we lived happily ever after. Which goes to show: you can't believe all the gossip you hear.

Gated Living

WE'VE BEEN IN SOUTH FLORIDA FOR A MONTH and I'm delighted with the weather and the place so far. Except when it comes to driving on the right-hand side of the road.

Stay right. I can't get the hang of this, dear God. The car seats nine people, designed for a huge family, but Jimmy thought it was the safest vehicle on the road. At least it's automatic. And the windows are tinted for protection against the sun, so people can't see me muttering to myself to *stay right*.

Why did I decide to come out this early? I'm stuck in the early-morning high-school traffic, wondering why the hell these people give their sixteen-year-old children cars. Are they mad? No, just American.

There's a cop car ahead. I must try to look like I know what I'm doing. I *do* know what I'm doing; I just don't know how to drive on the wrong side of the road. The air conditioner is on high, but I am drenched in sweat. Why am I afraid? This is simply a drive around the area, a practice run.

We live in a neighbourhood of forty houses, all curved around a man-made lake so that the back yard of each opens up onto the water. Ours is a single-storey; Ma would be unimpressed. She thinks you've only arrived if you live in a house with stairs. Our houses are perfect and clean, with only slight variations in the colour schemes. We have identical mail boxes, at a cost of $350 each. In our front gardens there are pretty mini-palm trees. They arrive fully grown, automatic additions like the grass and the garage doors. We subscribe to the same gardening service and the same pool-cleaning service.

Our neighbours are all white; I'm the only brown-skinned person around who isn't an employee. I'm thinking of learning Spanish, because it's becoming more and more embarrassing for me not to know it. Everyone thinks I'm playing white when I say, "No Spanish, just English. Inglés." I've learnt to nod knowingly as the woman at the bakery chats to me in Spanish. I just point out the cookies I want and smile. She could be discussing her last operation – the blood, the gall-stones in a jar – or her indulgence in bestiality, and all I do is smile and point and nod.

Sometimes I walk around the neighbourhood, wave to the black security guard at the entrance to the neighbourhood. No one can get in or out without signing in, without going past him, but I can't remember his name. There are security cameras lining the roads, for our protection. In the summer mornings, everything is still, quiet. It feels like I am on the set of a movie, without any dialogue.

Pregnancy Cravings

VISITING THE MAGIC KINGDOM, I BECOME A CHILD AGAIN, stepping into the life-size covers of my fairytale books. But something is missing. I find myself wishing I could share these Disney visits with a child. *My* child.

I try to ignore the cliché of the ticking biological clock and redirect my energies into a postgraduate degree (the working title for my dissertation is "Gold is the Fairest of All: Colour and Materialism in Fairytales"), but nothing will curb my yearning for a baby. The problem is that I can't get pregnant. The white-coated doctors in my adopted land of sour milk and stolen honey are still trying to figure out what's wrong.

Jimmy says we could always adopt, and tells me, "Don't worry babe, I'll be your baby forever." Are all men idiots? I don't want Jimmy to be my baby, I don't want to call him my precious pumpkin pie, my snoopy, my cookie or, worse, Daddy, like those creepy middle-aged women with stiff hair who talk to their child-substitute poodles in little-girl voices and ask them to bring Daddy's slippers.

My life has become a battle, an internal struggle. I'm helping Jimmy with his tax – I have a flair for numbers; I think it's got to do with having grown up in a babbie shop. (In fact, I strongly recommend that school-going children should be sent to work in a babbie shop: they'd never have problems with their multiplication timetables or general arithmetic, especially if they had a father like mine, who, if you messed up the change, would give you a fast klap to the head.) But all I can think about while I'm calculating Jimmy's returns is being pregnant. Wearing multicoloured tents and gaining a hundred kilos. I want a baby!

Jimmy does his best. He indulges in solitary pleasure in the bathroom, fantasising about me, he says, and I keep his tadpoles warm between my thighs while we drive to the hospital. They count his offerings and tell us Jimmy's boys are too damned slow, and that there are too few of them.

This starts us off on a round of endless hospital visits, with Jimmy squirting his DNA into test tube after test tube, and me, legs in stirrups, the undignified recipient of his lab-cleansed sperm. The romance of it all makes me want to weep.

What a twist of fate. We'd always been so keen on not getting pregnant, arming ourselves with pills and rubber and implants, and now, sans contraception, nothing is happening! Always, regular as clockwork, blood on the toilet seat, every full moon for a year. Jimmy says it's time to move on, it's time to adopt, but it doesn't feel right yet.

One night Jimmy's up watching American football, surely the most mind-numbing of all the dull sports men have developed, and I'm reading a book on spells – research – when it hits me.

Six weeks later, I'm pregnant. Jimmy says there's no way it was some flaky spell; it's the trips to the hospital that have paid off. But I know better.

....

Spell for a Baby Girl

1 ovulation kit

1 gold candle

1 red candle

1 silver candle

½ cup extra-virgin olive oil

1 red rose in full bloom with thorns

matches

Once you have read and followed the directions on the ovulation kit, and you know it is your most fertile time, prepare each candle carefully. Massage the oil gently into each candle from base to wick.

Next, arrange the three candles in a triangle. The top should be the red candle, the bottom left silver, and the bottom right gold. Prick your thumb with the thorn of the rose and squeeze three drops of blood onto the petals. Place the rose in the centre of the candle triangle.

Chant the following words: "Sweet as rose may be, powerful as thorn, a healthy baby girl from me shall be born." Picture your child's spirit rising to meet your body, like the rose germinating in the earth's rich soil before unfolding to the sky. When you are ready, snuff out the candles and place the rose under your mattress before making love. Remember to remove the rose the next day, because sleeping on a withered flower will make you grow old before your time.

. . . .

Manifestation

I'M TWENTY-SIX WEEKS PREGNANT AND ALL I DO IS vomit and think of Ma and Salena and home, until I find myself packing my bags and booking a ticket to Cape Town at 3 am one humid morning.

Jimmy thinks it's sweet. I want to be near my mommy for the birth of my daughter. But I know it doesn't make sense, that it's purely hormonal. Ma only likes me now because I live far away from her and have a wealthy white husband. And Ma's useless in a crisis. She says she can't stand the sight of blood. I find this highly suspect. Any woman who says "I faint at the sight of blood" is talking utter crap. I mean, what about all that blood that flows out of your body every month for about forty years?

Of course it makes sense for me to be near Salena. She knows all about babies, and she's a natural-born mother. Ma made her look after me when she was barely ten. I often speak to Salena on the phone before I fall asleep, as her day is dawning. After these talks my dreams are filled with our imagined adventures together. I wonder if we would have been as close if I had stayed in Cape Town. Maybe the distance has forged a stronger friendship.

Jimmy drops me off at the airport and we have a long lingering goodbye. We'll be apart for six weeks, and I'm ambivalent about the absence. Part of me wants him to suffer the thrills of my half-hourly trips to the toilet, and another part of me is delighted to be free of his endless talk of foetal development. If he brings home another baby magazine with a happy smiling pregnant woman on the cover I may have to commit mariticide.

As the plane takes off, the sun lights up the cabin, warming it. I feel like a biscuit in an oven, browning to perfection. A gingerbread girl. Is this what my baby feels like, cooking away inside of me? Suddenly the nausea that was supposed to stop at twelve weeks, according to those cheerful magazines, hits me. OH MY GOD. I vomit in my sick bag, and then in the bag of the unfortunate soul next to me, and finally I have used up all the bags in my row and the flight attendants have stopped smiling at me. I sleep for a while, until I'm woken up by the smell of airline food and I promptly throw up into the closest thing, my skirt.

Then I'm in Cape Town, so jet-lagged and stinky that I barely recognise myself, let alone Salena, who has come with Ma to fetch me. I'm going to stay with her in her new home in Pinelands, near the hospital. It's a good distance from Ma's new Claremont townhouse. I'm not completely hormonally deranged. Me and Ma under one roof? Not a chance. We can chat on the phone.

I sleep for two nights and days, waking up intermittently to pee and drink water and then, five minutes later, to throw it up. Salena's guest toilet is really clean. Even under the brim. Her toilet could star in one of those advertisements for toilet cleaners – the "After" version.

Salena looks different, and I'm picking up vibes between her and Zain. I start to wonder if I should rather have stayed in a hotel.

Two weeks after my arrival in Cape Town, I begin to get excruciating back pains. I don't want to bother Salena, so I haul myself off to the obstetrician she's arranged for me. The OB-GYN looks about eleven years old and speaks with a heavy Afrikaans accent. She tells me that my back pain, excruciating as it is, is normal, and once she establishes it's my first pregnancy, I am dismissed as being a hysterical first-time mommy. She tells me to go for physiotherapy.

So, with my tail between my legs, I slink back to Salena's. The pain terrorises me all night long. The next morning, after a handful of Panados, I make the appointment with the physiotherapist. Salena arranges for a neighbour to take me there, and the physiotherapist woman tells me I'd know if I was in labour. She proceeds to attach wires to my body, and while I think she plans on electrocuting me, it seems she's only going to give me electrical jolts. They don't work. I try to survive that night by rubbing my lower back against the wall and taking more Panado's. Neither helps. In the middle of the night, Salena and an elderly Peanut Butter keep me company. Salena makes me toast and tea, and we play Snakes & Ladders. I lose, even though I cheat.

The pain is intolerable, and this time Salena calls an ambulance. I feel like a fraud. I keep telling her the doctor said I was a melodramatic first-time mother, and that I should just grin and bear it. But Salena will hear none of it.

I am pushed into an examination room by the ambulance attendant and Salena goes into the waiting room. A nurse begins to examine me, and I am hooked up to a machine. This one spews out paper and beeps contentedly. The nurse is wearing a pale green uniform, and she smiles all the time. I like her. She says, "Mommy, you're definitely in labour."

My heart stops. I know, because I can't hear the machine beeping.

"Okay," I agree, albeit reluctantly. "Bring on the drugs."

"You're nine centimetres dilated," she tells me. "Just one more centimetre and baby will be ready. It's too late for drugs." Now there's something Jimmy's pregnancy magazines never mentioned – I thought it was never too late for drugs.

The nurse is serene and explains the procedure to me with gentle words. She stands on my left, cradles my head with her right hand, and cups my left leg under my knee with her left arm. But the baby, who has been letting me know for two weeks that she wants to be born, is pissed off. The monitors start beeping angrily. Baby's cord is around her neck. A doctor I have never seen before arrives. He chats to me but I can't hear a word. I see a silvery needle in his hand and notice his manicured nails. Then, casually, like he's using kitchen scissors to cut the skin off a breast of chicken, he slices my vagina open. My brain reminds me that Jimmy's magazines called this an episiotomy. What a lyrical word for such an ugly deed. Out pops my child, and they slip her into my left armpit where she nestles in a spot that appears to have been designed with her in mind.

She looks at me vaguely and then, with more interest, at the play of light and shadow on the ceiling made by the cars driving past the window. She makes soundless noises with her mouth. She has no eyebrows, like Ma. Salena comes in, kisses my wet cheeks and whispers the azan in my daughter's right ear, before the nurse whisks her away. For a moment it feels like they have taken my left arm too.

I phone Jimmy as he's sitting down to a supper of home-delivered pizza, my favourite pregnancy meal. The line's bad, our voices echo and bounce against each other. But when he finally understands, his near-silent sniffs are more valuable to me than the most extravagant of his gifts.

Later I get to see her, my baby, Nazma, my star-child. She has a tube up her nose, other tubes are hooked up to her, machines are beeping, but she sleeps as if she invented the act. I cannot believe that outside of this room, this ward, this hospital, there is a spinning earth, with all its joys and horrors, because my world lies in an incubator.

Dreams of Sleep

I FANTASISE ABOUT SLEEP THE WAY MEN ARE SUPPOSED to think about sex all the time. I crave a night of uninterrupted sleep the way I craved chocolate before my period when I was a teenager. I long for my body to be mine, not to wake up ten times a night to feel little demanding hands clawing at my breasts for sustenance.

Since Nazma's birth I can't remember sleeping for more than an hour or two at a time. She's supposed to be sleeping through the night, according to her doctor and the baby magazines Jimmy still buys. But she doesn't read the magazines so she doesn't know she's falling short of her milestones. Often she screeches hysterically, ear-piercingly, for what seems to be no particular reason. She's not hungry, she's not wet, she's not cold. There is no obvious source to her despair.

Sometimes I dance with her, sometimes I coo lullabies. Sometimes I fantasise about placing a soft feathery pillow over her dewy skin, her eyes like open flowers, and just holding it there until she sleeps for a hundred years.

I'm an unnatural mother. I've never heard other moms wishing their children away. Maybe I'm becoming Ma.

When I'm close to despair I break into Jimmy's snores and he is instantly alert and inexplicably upbeat. He hugs her close to his chest and strolls around the room like he was born to the task. If only he could lactate. I leave them to it and find the dark smoothness of the couch and the comforting undemanding bodies of my cats Lily and Raven. All too soon it is time for another feed, and I force my gritty eyes as far open as they can go.

Jimmy gets home-help, Spanish-accented Gregoria, whose voice sounds like she's permanently on the verge of catching a heavy cold and who wears long dark dresses in a heavy fabric, with long sleeves, even in the Floridian heat, because she wanted to be a nun but her agnostic father wouldn't allow it. Instead she has made a career out of caring for other people's children. She says Nazma might be her last baby; she's searching for a cloister that will accept her although she is approaching her fortieth birthday. Nazma likes her. She naps in a sling against her body for hours, and I am free to sleep, but find it impossible to do so. I'm jealous of Gregoria's competence. But by the time Nazma turns a year old and Gregoria bakes her a gingerbread house birthday cake from scratch, I am prepared to bow to her domestic agility.

She takes control of the house and it preens under her attention. Even the taps sparkle in a way I never could get them to do. Gregoria hates crowds and goes shopping at midnight when the supermarket is near empty. I get used to her unpacking groceries in the early hours of the morning. She teaches Nazma to talk in English and Spanish. She takes all my favourite recipes and meticulously types them up and has them printed and bound into a book, protected by plastic sheets. Then she learns to cook them better than I ever could. Gradually the bits of my brain that Nazma has not turned to sludge reappear, and I go back to my neglected dissertation. Life is peaceful.

Fatherhood

She promised me her firstborn; I'd come to collect. I was happy, I was delighted, I was thrilled. I would have a child of my own to love and nurture, and protect. Some little being who would look up to me even if he outgrew me. I pictured us in front of the fire, him asleep in his crib, me smoking my little pipe, both of us content.

I expected her to kick up a fuss, and was surprised when she didn't.

"Ah, it's you. At last you've come for the child. Took your time, didn't you?" She glanced irritably at her wristwatch. "Yes, it's a girl. You said firstborn. You didn't specify gender. I don't suppose you have a wet-nurse yet? No? Well, that's fine, I have one. This here is Sarah, and her little one, Mimi. What? Well of course they'll have to go with you. She's only a few days old, she'll starve to death otherwise. Mimi? Yes, her too, she's Sarah's kid. Wet-nurses always have their own children, otherwise they wouldn't be wet-nurses. Yes, the babies are noisy. No, you don't get used to it. At least I haven't.

"The smell? Just a bit of baby pooh. You'll stop noticing it soon enough. Besides, she's breastfed; the smell would be worse if she were on formula. Which reminds me: these three bags contain her nappies. The other ten have her clothes – mostly presents. I haven't had time to sort them out, I thought you could do that. Then if you'll look out the window— What's that? Oh right, let me pick you up. My, you are a heavy fellow, aren't you? Anyway, that lot downstairs are the toys.

"The crying? Colic. Should go away in three or four months, or so the baby magazines claim. Sarah? No, dear, she's the wet-nurse, not the parent, you'll have to deal with all the other aspects: the bathing, the putting to sleep, the entertaining. And of course Sarah doesn't do the 3 am feed. She expresses breast milk the night before.

"Now, I've drawn up a schedule for each day of the week. Let's begin with Monday. That's your bowling night? Don't be ridiculous. No, there'll be none of that. You've got a child now: you need to be responsible. There'll be no more movie nights, no book club, no AA meetings, no full-moon spell nights. Listen, you wanted the child, now you've got to live with your decision. You made me promise. A verbal contract. What? You don't want the baby anymore? Well, I'm not sure if I do either."

Burial

MY BREASTS HAVE BEEN FEELING STRANGE FOR A WHILE: warm, and the skin has changed, like they're developing cellulite. At first I think it's hormonal. Even though Nazma's almost three years old, I imagine it is somehow linked to my pregnancy, or that I am pregnant again. I keep putting off seeing a doctor until the occasional twinge becomes pain.

Now I know. I have invasive breast cancer but it's been caught in the first stage. I'll need some form of surgery; a lumpectomy as the tumour is still small. They say I'll need radiation therapy as well.

I phone Salena, across time zones, mountains and oceans, until I am in her bedroom, at midnight, her time. I tell her why I need her to visit me. She thinks I'm catastrophising. But when she finally believes me, I hear her unspoken fears, and this unleashes my terror, as though I've rubbed the magic lamp in which it was imprisoned. I imagine her cradling the phone under her ear while her fingers caress the phone's cord, as though it were my one of my curls, and I'm comforted. She agrees to visit. I feel buoyant. Even though Jimmy has been wonderful, I need my sister.

Then Salena is with me. She holds my hand in the hospital's corridors and she sits with me at night in the hospital's muggy garden listening to the frogs. The doctors have asked me to stay on another day or two, like they're hotel managers who can't bear to let me, a favourite guest, end her vacation with them.

At night, after Jimmy has left the hospital and my spacious private room is covered in moonlight, she tells me stories of our daadi, who died a year after I was born.

I know my dead grandmother only by the shiny bangles my mother wears on her wrists, bangles Daadi left for Salena, but which my mother claimed as her own. The bangles were all that was left of my grandmother's jewellery. The other pieces went missing mysteriously, according to Salena.

Salena says Daadi told Ma that one day she had put on all her jewellery in readiness for a wedding, but as she went outside a great black bird swooped out of the sky and ripped the jewellery off her fingers and throat. She said the bird had the face of a demon, but she recited her Quls and the bird grew smaller and smaller, until it turned to dust, along with her jewels.

She lost every piece except for the bangles on her wrists, which nothing, not even soap and water, not even magic, could get off, because she hadn't taken them off since our great-grandmother, her mother-in-law, put them on her skinny bride-wrists.

Salena says Ma cut the bangles off the corpse of our grandmother, and the 22-carat gold was so soft, the knife slid through it like butter, slicing through each of the dozen bangles. Six from each arm. Ma had the bangles repaired the very next day, and then added them to her own heavy arms, already filled with jingly bracelets. The first time I saw an American Christmas tree, all garishly decorated, I was reminded of my mother – a Christmas tree in court shoes, too weighed down by decorations to ever move freely.

But there's another story about how our granny's missing jewellery went missing. It happened in a park.

It was an ugly council park, protected from the invasion of certain children by its metal green-linked fence and its WHITES ONLY signs. I can remember peering at the park from behind the fence, but I never dared go in. Of course Salena, with her fair skin, could pass, as could Daadi.

On the morning that Daadi's jewellery went missing, it was a brilliantly sunny day. The unwelcome children gawked wistfully through the fence at the deserted black-tyre swings, and the park's two adult occupants. The first was a plump, elderly woman, dressed in a gaudy scarlet sari and seated on a green park bench. The children recognised her. She was the motjie, Aunty Bilqis from Hanif Paruk General Dealers, the corner babbie shop on Albert Road. She snuck them homemade burfi, Sunrise toffees and Chappies bubblegum when her stout son left the café for his afternoon nap.

The second occupant, known only as Poison-Parkie, was the poor-white park keeper whose job it was to care for the grass and feed the goldfish which swam fatly in the murky waters of the park's immense fishpond. The children hated him; he always chased after them with his spindly legs and his brown stick.

Poison-Parkie stopped weeding the perfect grass carpet when he noticed the woman. Milky skin. Straight hair. She must be white. But, still, she was wearing one of those funny dresses, and you could see the bare, fair, fleshy rolls of her stomach. Sies! Now he recognised her. How dared she sit on his bench? Who did she think she was? Just because she could pass for white. He heard the children laughing behind him.

"Voetsek," Poison-Parkie shouted at them and they ran off, shrieking.

He turned back to look at the woman. She was no longer sitting on the bench, but standing near the fishpond. He watched as she threw something into the water. It landed with a splash.

"Hey, you! Lady!" Poison-Parkie hated cleaning the slimy fishpond and now here was this bladdy non-white woman throwing things in the water.

Poison-Parkie marched towards her. Just as he opened his mouth to shout at her again, he saw her undo a red and yellow collar from her neck and drop it into the pond. He froze. Next, she poured the rings off her fingers into the willing, waiting water.

The old woman didn't even look at him, just turned and walked away. She must be bladdy mad, he thought. He knew that babbie women wore real jewellery, not the fake stuff his wife bought from OK Bazaars in Adderley Street when they went shopping on Saturday mornings. It was like winning the jackpot. He'd make a fortune. Much more than the pennies he got when stupid courting couples threw their money into the pond on wasteful wishes.

Poison-Parkie was thigh-high in green water, trying to retrieve the jewellery with thirsty fingers. He had one gold ring, but the bigger piece, the necklace, was eluding him, drawing him down, further into the water. His head went under.

The children snuck in. Each to a designated target. A black swing. A red slide. A yellow seesaw.

In the pond that he had neglected for too long, Poison-Parkie's feet slid out from under him, and his head knocked against the grey, concrete wall. Slimy green water turned ruby red, like the jewellery he would never reach. He heard the children's giggles bubbling faintly in his ears, saw his world turn black.

Bilqis Paruk paused at the gate. Should she go back to get her jewellery? Keep it for her grandchildren, Salena or Faruk? No, she wouldn't. She wanted to teach her son Hanif a lesson after he'd asked her for the trinkets to give to his wife, as though they were his due, as though she owed him anything. After all, what had she lost? Just a few worldly possessions, duniya things. She strolled out of the park, the children's laughter following her home.

Of course, Hanif hit the roof when he couldn't find his mother's jewellery, but by then Bilqis had moved on.

I love Salena's stories; I could listen to her for hours, but eventually I am free to go home. Nazma greets me at the door, lugging what looks like a bird cage behind her. Perched inside it is a giant lizard. Her birthday present from Gregoria. I pretend enthusiasm.

In my bedroom, I settle into my extra-sized bed with its view of the back garden, the pool and the lake beyond the fence. I've decided that what I need is a sacrifice to heal my sick body, and while I can't bring myself to agree to an animal slaughter, I have the next best thing – a mink coat Jimmy bought in a moment of lavish forgetfulness. While I'm not exactly an animal activist, I am vegetarian, and I wouldn't be caught dead in fur, not even fake fur. So I tell Salena we have to bury the coat in the garden as a means of atoning for my sins, real or imagined. Salena looks dubious but is prepared to indulge me.

I lounge back in one of the pool chairs and watch Salena dig.

She's chosen a spot near the fence, which separates the pool from the glossy man-made lake. Through the links in the fence, I can see three toads observing Salena's progress, occasionally croaking and ribbeting encouragement.

I go into the kitchen to soak some bread for them. When I get back, Salena is nearly done with the digging. I surreptitiously push the bread through the fence. I don't want the neighbours to report my transgression to the home owners' association. Salena tells me to stop feeding the toads. She says I'm destroying the local ecosystem: they should be eating insects, not bleached white flour. Of course she's right, but I feed them anyway.

The shallow grave is complete and I dig out the incense sticks which I burn every Thursday night, the way I was taught to do as a child. The smoke makes Salena cry. I lean against her for support, hold her hand, and we offer up a prayer for the souls of the dead minks. I wonder if they were Everglade minks. If so, then at least they've come home. The toads continue to croon, and in the encroaching dusk we can hear an alligator crying out for a mate.

From inside the house the smell of the potato samoosas Gregoria is frying wafts out to us, a subtle invitation to eat, to live, to pray. I hope she's made dhania chutney too.

I swear the burial helps, because I go into remission.

. . . .

Dhania Chutney

¼ cup lemon juice

¼ cup water

4 bunches dhania, washed and coarsely chopped

2 tsp fresh ginger, finely chopped

2 red chillies, chopped

1 tsp honey

¼ tsp black pepper

½ tsp salt

Combine the lemon juice, water and half a cup of dhania in a blender. Blend until pureed, and then add another half cup of dhania. Repeat until all the dhania has been pureed. Add the rest of the ingredients and blend until perfectly smooth. You could add more salt or honey if desired. You can eat it immediately or store it in the fridge for a while. Delicious with samoosas but also good on toast.

....

Waiting

IT'S NAZMA'S FIFTH BIRTHDAY, AND WE'VE DECIDED to come to Cape Town for an extended holiday. I can't imagine moving back here forever, but I miss Salena. It'll be fun to be in closer proximity, just for a few months. I even miss Ma. Sort of. Okay, I have grave doubts about staying in the same city as Ma, but she is older now. Maybe she's mellowed.

We've been travelling almost twenty-four hours, and this dreary wait at Cape Town International is not endearing me to my sister. Salena must have forgotten we're arriving today although she insisted on coming to fetch us now that she's learning to drive. I've put Nazma back in her harness, and she's barking at all the passers-by, while simultaneously chewing on the cookies she refuses to leave home without, and clutching the weird blonde doll Gregoria gave her as a birthday gift. For a woman who still occasionally makes noises about joining a nunnery, Gregoria has a strange taste in gifts. Last year she gave Nazma a Spiderman gun that oozed goo, which was an improvement on the previous year's Komodo dragon. No matter what Jimmy says, I know he convinced her to get that creature.

I like missing Jimmy. I like the way he woos me over the phone and I adore the letters he writes me. I fall in love with him all over again after a long absence. When he's around all the time he tends to get on my nerves. Even now, after all these years, he still wraps himself around me at night as if he's tinfoil and I'm a piece of leftover pumpkin pie.

Departing Florida, I was subjected to another so-called random search at the airport. My Muslim surname must have triggered off the computer's alarm bells. It's not my fault; it's my father's surname. I should have taken Jimmy's simple English last name, but I kept saying, "No way will I change my name! We're getting married; he's not adopting me." See where my feminist principles have got me!

The flight has exhausted me and, thanks to Nazma, the dungarees I'm wearing are covered in chocolate and spilt coffee and coke. On flights before Nazma was born, I used to sit in a window seat, plug in my headphones, pop a sleeping pill and fall asleep over a book. Travelling with a small human who needs the toilet at thirty-minute intervals has changed flying forever.

I hope Salena gets here before Nazma asks for the toilet. We've got too much luggage to make a public bathroom trip anything but an ordeal. Surely Salena hasn't forgotten about me. I am her only sister, after all. Maybe she's had an accident. Maybe her car won't start because she's left the lights on. No, that's something I would do, especially now that I have Nazma to distract me.

What am I going to do? I look up to see a strange woman smiling at me. I smile back automatically and my eyes slide over and past her until my brain catches up. Salena!

No way.

Hair short, with coppery highlights, styled, no longer in a neat bun, swishing across rosy cheeks and fringing shiny eyes. Straight away, I know. Salena's in love!

Yours Faithfully

Dear Ms Hood

You don't know me, but I've been watching you for years, since you were a little girl, all through high school when you had that rebellious phase with the biker boyfriend. Yes, I know there were many other boyfriends, but he scared me the most – I know you loved him. Then you left for college, and my heart broke. I thought you were lost to me forever. So imagine my delight when I heard that you'd returned, that you'd graduated as a vet. I am filled with pride at your accomplishment. I admire you so much.

I know I must sound like a common stalker, but I don't have an altar to you in my lair, the walls of my home are not covered with photographs of you. I carry you in my heart and in my head. I wake each morning with your name on my lips, dripping like drool from my jaws. I know I'm risking ridicule with all these revelations, but my therapist says it is important that I tell you everything.

Yes, I have loved you from afar all these years, from the shadows of the woods. I first saw you one day when you were a little girl, taking a basket of goodies to your sick grandmother. My mouth watered at the sight of you. It was all I could do not to gobble you up right there and then, but I thought, Why not follow you and have your granny, too?

But by the time you got to your grandmother's house, something in my consciousness had shifted. I knew I loved you, but that I did not have to consume you and your relations. I started therapy. I stopped chasing the three little pigs (that was part of my self-destructive youth). I became vegetarian. I noticed you always had your hair covered, and I wondered if you were Muslim. I spent years studying Islam in the hope that this would impress you.

I understand I have little to offer you, aside from my sharp teeth, my warm fur, my keen night-time vision, my undying devotion, and the knowledge that grey wolves mate for life, unlike the boyfriends of your past. I am hoping that as a vet you will not be adverse to an inter-species relationship. I am praying you will accept my invitation. A cup of coffee, next full moon. Ten minutes of your life, a chance to woo you: that is all I ask. No strings attached. Feel free to discuss it with your mother and grandmother – they are your pack, they have wisdom.

I await your response. However, if you choose not to reply I will understand. I will be unhappy, but I will understand. You owe me nothing for loving you, it has been my opportunity for growth.

Yours faithfully
Wolfie

Driving Ma

Now that I'm on this extended holiday, Ma seems to think it's only right that I become her personal chauffer. Why did I imagine I could come to Cape Town and live outside of Ma's freaky control?

Today she wants me to take her to the city. She wants to visit a kramat but she won't drive into town because of the taxis. Ma says she's told The Prune time and again to go to the kramat to get rid of her bad luck, but Polla won't listen. Polla's always having car troubles, money troubles, man troubles.

On the drive here, Ma was waxing eloquent about my big sister. Apparently, she's forgiven her for divorcing Zain, because now Salena takes Ma out once a week for tea. Which, Ma says, is something that never happened when Salena was married to "that man".

At the kramat, I park the car close to the kerb and Ma goes inside the burial room to pray. Papa never allowed her to visit kramats because he said she was praying to the saint, instead of directly to Allah, which made her no better than a worshipper of idols. Ma denied this but could never make Papa believe her. Papa didn't get that Ma loves the ritual of lighting an incense stick and the peace of prayer, particularly because, she tells me, as a woman she's been made to feel uncomfortable in a mosque.

I sit in the car until the heat forces me out. Behind the square of the kramat's resting place is a girls' school, and in the hazy distance I can see a few uniformed figures throwing balls about. A door in the building behind me opens, and two white-haired women in flowery dresses make their way haltingly towards a wooden bench, where they gingerly collapse and the dusty smell of talcum powder reaches out to me. They clasp each other's hand. I wonder if Salena and I will grow old together like that.

Ma's back, looking optimistic. Have her prayers been answered? We get into the car. She says she understands why we have to pray five times a day. It was Allah's way of getting the dirty Arab men to wash regularly, and forcing them to focus on something besides chasing women. I'm beginning to like Ma.

Cleaning

MA'S CUPBOARD OPENS AND HER SMELL WAFTS OUT: a heavy floral scent. I remember when these smells were a comfort to the child-me, when I would lie, pimply with chicken pox, my nose buried in her nightgown.

The week before, I went to visit Papa's grave – for the first time ever. That day I got as far as the dusty, gravelly parking lot, before my courage almost deserted me, but I persevered. I sat in the car, clutching the flowers I'd bought at Woolies, already wilting in the heat. I didn't know you could purchase bunches of the stuff outside the cemetery for a fraction of the price. I turned the car back on and put the air-conditioner on full blast.

I don't see the point of flowers on graves. I don't see the point of graves. I plan on being cremated. Ma said she would never allow this. What would people say? It never occurred to her she'd die before me. Ma believed she was immortal, that dying was something other people did.

Ma warned me about the grave cleaners hanging around the cemetery. Not that she ever went there herself; the man she hired to maintain my father's grave told her. He said there were men, mostly illegal immigrants, who made money cleaning the graves for visitors. So when I got there, I wasn't surprised to see men walking around with little shovels. They looked creepy in their white coats, like living ghouls. I wondered if they lived in the cemetery, like the squatters in Cairo who have moved into the graveyards for lack of urban space.

Eventually I got out of the car, only to be surrounded by a group of grave guards. But I'd come prepared. I was covered from head to toe in a burqa, with horizontal slits for my eyes. Of course this meant I had no peripheral driving vision, which had made the drive here somewhat dicey.

Salena had said Papa's grave would be easy to find – against the wall, seventh row from the front. As I searched, an insistent guard followed me, nattering incomprehensibly. From the safety of my black shroud, I stuck my tongue out at him and shook my head vehemently from side to side. It didn't help. He was undeterred, and followed me until I reached the meticulously kept grave.

Ma was surely getting her money's worth. There was a suitably severe headstone, all covered in pretty roses and carnations, displaying Papa's name, date of birth and date of death. I felt slightly faint crouching there in the 32-degree heat and my heavy, black attire. I didn't know what to think. All I could see in my head were visions of my father beating Salena until bruises like violets covered her pallid skin.

Then, as I turned to go, I noticed the name on the gravestone next to Papa's. Mrs Julayga Slamang. I looked around. In the grave behind him lay Gamiet Salie. My father had Malay neighbours! I choked on hysterical silent laughter. I searched further. Parker, Rawoot, Narkar, Karjiker. Indian village stalwarts buried in between Matthews and Fredericks.

The proximity of his bones to those Malays must be killing him all over again, daily. I'll confess: I went back to my car much lighter. Now all I can think about is that Ma will be Papa's neighbour, too. I wonder if they'll get along better in death than in life.

We don't know what happened. Salena found her in the lounge. *Oprah* playing on the TV, a cup of tea next to her, as cold as her skin. Salena says she felt bad interrupting Ma watching TV, knowing how much she loved Oprah. So Salena watched the show along with Ma and when the credits began to roll she phoned me.

I know I should cry. It's the right thing to do.

· ·

Potpourri

4 cups rose petals

1 tsp powdered aniseed

1 tsp powdered allspice

1 tsp powdered nutmeg

6 long cinnamon sticks, coarsely broken

1 tsp powdered ginger

¼ cup whole cloves

1 tsp ground cinnamon

2 vanilla pods, cut into 2 cm pieces

20 drops essential rose oil

1 cup coarse sea salt

Cut flowers may wilt quickly in the summer heat, and transforming them into potpourri is a way of lengthening their too-short lives and making them productive instead of merely decorative. Mix all of the ingredients together in a large bowl and place it in a room or in the middle of a house that needs its spirits lifted, particularly after a bereavement.

· ·

Different Tastes

I was alone, for a short time, while Hansel went outside to play with his new collection of pearls, rich rubies, diamonds and other jewels. I wanted to make sure she was dead. When I opened the oven door, I found her, the tough old bird, already overcooked, but still tempting. And I thought: Just a nibble, a suck. After all, she was going to eat Hansel. She tasted burnt, but her skin crackled pleasurably on my tongue, and I chewed delicately as her once-solid flesh became mine.

At home there was much rejoicing, and we three settled into a comfortable life, no one mentioning our stepmother. It's strange, now that I think about it after all these years: we never asked father how she died. Simply celebrated her absence. Had he killed her in a fit of guilt over dumping us in the forest? Did she run away with a man who could feed her? Did she die of hunger? What's even odder is that we never blamed him for our abandonment. It was always her fault; she was the villain in our story.

We delighted in the presence of the abundant food. Each morning, I cooked an enormous breakfast: porridge, scrambled eggs, fried bread, flapjacks sweating honey and cream. Hansel insisted on elevenses: triangles of cheese-and-tomato sandwiches, and samoosas with dhania chutney. Then lunch. Soup and salad for starters. A leg of lamb, curried chicken and basmati rice, fish almost swimming in butter and lemon juice. A pudding of yellow custard and brown syrupy fruit. I drew the line at cooking supper. They ate leftovers or cornflakes with thick slices of banana. Father grew a belly. Hansel spurted into a long-limbed teenager and took up weight-lifting; he grew as sleek as a forest cat. But I found the food unsatisfying: often, I left my plate untouched. I had other longings.

Then Father sickened and died. The doctor said it was an extreme case of heartburn. I convinced Hansel that a cremation would be less expensive. Now that he was wealthy, he hated to spend any of our ill-gotten gains. It's funny how having lots of money can make a man stingy. He found pleasure in playing with his jewels, but he hated converting them into hard cash and spending the stuff – even on food. I said it would be cheaper if I burnt Father myself. Hansel left me to it, and I held back a thigh, to roast and season at my leisure. That hit the spot.

Without Father to bind us, Hansel and I drifted apart. I saw him watching our neighbour all the time, a moronic girl, always asking Hansel to help her get rid of mice, tweaking my nose as though we were friends.

Hansel and I divided the remaining loot, with him taking the lion's share – I didn't care. I needed to move out. I went back to her gingerbread house, threw out her ashes, put potpourri in all the rooms, and restored the place to its former scrumptious glory. I took up cake-baking to cover my living costs, to keep me entertained and busy. I'm a perfectionist: I've been known to throw out a perfectly good sponge if there's a little hollow in the centre, one that only I can see.

We wait, the always-warm oven and me. To hear some stray, small person's juicy-pink lips, someone's lickable white milk teeth nibbling at my chocolate windows.

When Salena was born, she had black hair, dark as midnight, and eyes grey-blue as a turbulent sea. Her mother, while disappointed at the birth of a daughter, was glad that at least the girl looked white. Imagine her displeasure when, within weeks, Salena's eyes turned green, her hair a rusty brown. At least her skin stayed fair.

Hafsa soon grew irritated with the child, wishing her away as she prepared for another pregnancy, a replacement for the disappointment.

Salena learnt early that neglect was preferable to being beaten, and that submission ensured neglect, so as a little girl she bit her tongue and cut her flesh until her body became perfectly silent.

In fact, Salena stayed silent for several decades. But she did speak up, eventually.

Let me tell you her story.

Salena's Tale

Cango Delights

SALENA'S FATHER, HANIF PARUK, HAS A NEW VOLVO, and they're leaving Cape Town to visit the Cango Caves in Oudtshoorn. There is an air of festivity in the car that not even the bruises on Salena's waxen arms can diminish. Faruk sits in the front, next to their father, and Salena and her mother, Hafsa, have the back seat. The car smells of padkos, especially the garlic chutney Hanif insists Hafsa spread on all his sandwiches, no matter what the filling. He even eats it with peanut butter.

No one speaks as Hanif concentrates on driving. Occasionally he lets Faruk change gears – it's never too early for a boy to learn how to drive.

They stop at a garage for petrol and for Hafsa to use the toilet. Hafsa comes back, adjusting her scarf and complaining about the state of the toilets. She tells Salena that at the next garage she must ask for the toilet key so that they can be sure to get the ones to the white toilets.

Salena, seated in the back seat, shifts until she can see her face in the car's rear-view mirror. She looks at her skin, chalky white, her eyes the colour of marbles. Her hair, in its two plaits, has an auburn glow, and her nose is short and narrow. This face, this reflection, dooms her to playing white on family excursions, or whenever her parents demand it.

She is the third in the queue at the Caves. If she fails, she knows she'll get another hiding with the belt, or her father's other favourite, the wooden spoon. Ahead of her are a mother and three children. The children, two boys and a girl, turn to stare at Salena. Her cheeks redden. Can they see she's not white?

She looks away, then back. The children are barefoot. The boys have shorn hair, showing their pink scalps, and the girl's hair is blonde, waist-length and horribly knotted. Their faces are smeared with strawberry jam and dirt.

When it's her turn, she smiles politely at the woman selling tickets and asks for tickets for two children and two grown-ups, in what Hafsa calls "high English". The woman smiles back, hands her the tickets, and says she is lucky; this is the last tour of the day.

She goes back to the car, parked out of sight of the ticket counter, and gives her father the tickets. In her absence, Salena's mother has added more white powder to her face, so her dark skin glints grey. She's freshened her pale pink lipstick too, and removed her scarf. Her thick black hair, most of it artificial, is arranged on top of her head like Elizabeth Taylor's.

Off they go, up the path. They are the last to join the queue. Hanif hands over the tickets to the collector. He scrutinises each member of the family.

"This tour is for whites only."

Her mother's face, under its pale guise, begins to melt in the rays of the afternoon sun.

"Go, before you get into trouble, just go! I want to get home early for a change."

The family turn as one, back to the car. As they drive away, Faruk is crying. Salena can't understand why. Their father hardly ever hits him. She feels queasy. She puts her head out of the car window and leaves a trail of padkos in the dusty road.

· ·

Masala Peanuts

½ cup chana flour, sifted
¼ cup rice flour, sifted
1½ tsp chilli powder
salt to taste
1 cup salted roasted peanuts
5 tbsp water
oil for frying

Mix the sifted chana flour, rice flour, chilli powder and salt together in a bowl. Stir in the peanuts and slowly add 4 or 5 tablespoons of water. Heat the oil in a pan and drop the peanut mixture into the hot oil. Separate the peanuts that clump together. Deep-fry over medium heat until the peanuts are golden brown. Allow to cool and place in an airtight container. The perfect snack for long car trips.

· ·

A Visit to the Beach

THE MIDNIGHT WAVES WASH OVER SALENA's feet as she lies on her back in the sand, watching the full moon, a sallow reflection of the sun. She wishes the moon, her namesake, could reach down and pull her up into its heavens.

At the library, she read that a man had walked on the moon, and in her last year of primary school she was taught that the moon affects the tides, that it exerts a pull on the seas, on water.

The beach is Salena's refuge from her father's rages. She knows the routine: grab Zuhra and her bottle as well as a handful of the biscuits her mother keeps on a shelf near the back door, and run. Across the main road, past the Catholic school, to the stony beach.

She hears the giggles of her two-year-old sister. The baby is trying to catch the white foam on the black waves with her left hand while holding her milk bottle high in her right one. Little Zuhra doesn't understand that people don't visit the beach at this time. She does not know yet that water is treacherous, that there are sea monsters living in the dark, watching from below. She does not know that the butter-yellow midnight moon is natural light to predators, and should not be witnessed by children on a dark beach.

Salena recalls, as a tiny child, perhaps as little as Zuhra is now, being protected in her daadi's arms, while around her the storm that is her father raged. Now with her grandmother gone, she is her sister's rescuer. Salena tries to rise, but her arms are as limp as the seaweed strewn on the sand, her body as fluid as the water.

She collapses back onto the sand, spreads her arms out wide, and gazes up at the opaque clouds moving across the moon's crust. Her hand closes around the sharp edge of a broken shell. She tightens her fist around it until the skin yields, and the moon is witness to the blood mixing with sand.

Coke Float Dreams

SALENA TREADS SOFTLY ON THE STONE PAVEMENT in the dark morning, past the row of cottages and storefronts that separates her father's house from his cornershop, Hanif Paruk General Dealer.

The street lamp throws its bleak light on the tiny keyholes of the padlocks that guard the shop each night. The keys grate, opening a shadowy world of sweets and cigarettes. She reaches for the broom to sweep away the musty night, readying herself for the deliveries of hot bread and icy milk.

She thinks of her parents, undisturbed, asleep beneath their mirrored gudri. It has been her job to open the shop, every day, for two years now, ever since her thirteenth birthday.

That birthday morning had been a gloomy winter one, too. She'd heard the black telephone ringing at seven o'clock, as she was ironing her school pinafore, dark red cotton, dampened to smooth the iron's path. Her father had answered, and then, with a surprised, silent scowl, handed the receiver to her.

Her quivering ear heard a boy's voice wishing her happy birthday, a short laugh, a click as he replaced the receiver. She turned to face her parents' glares.

Later, at school, Mrs Goosen pinched her twice for not concentrating, and made her sit at her desk during break, writing, "I will listen to my teacher, I will listen to my teacher," one hundred times.

That afternoon she walked into the house and sniffed the air for her mother's mood, heard her twelve-year-old brother's squeaky voice tormenting her cat, then felt her eyes brimming even before her mother's words.

"You think now you're in high school you can become ougat? I spoke to your father, and we decided no more school for you! If you're old enough for boyfriends, you're old enough to work in the shop full-time. Your father's right: you'll only bring shame on us."

Two years later, she is an expert at her duties. When the bread and milk arrive, she counts the loaves and hands over payment, and dries the sweat off the glass milk bottles. Mr Paul arrives for his usual three "losse Stuyvesants" and his customary "Don't forget to smile" good-bye. He's followed by the local sweet-factory workers, the smell of sugar cloying on their clothes. Then, before the school bell rings out from across the road, runny-nosed children hurry in to buy "bread on the book and a piece of butter too".

Finally, the factory workers have left to clock in, the children are imprisoned behind school desks, and it is time to get ready for the next round of buying, at teatime.

She divides the pink penny polony for sandwiches and boils eggs while she butters the rolls they will fill. Then she stocks the fridge with bottles of Coke and ginger beer, pumps paraffin into plastic bottles, unpacks boxes of chips and puts more cans of beans on the shelves.

As she works she thinks of Hafsa's casually dropped comment the previous night. "I think it's time we find a husband for you, before you disgrace us again. When you have your own children you'll see how difficult they can be – just you wait."

Her chores done, she glances out of the window and notices the moon, still visible in the morning sky. She thinks of her flimsy body stretching to encompass an unwanted stranger and shudders, and wraps her skinny arms around herself.

· ·

Coke Float

2 scoops vanilla ice-cream
250 ml Coke

Put two scoops of ice-cream into a tall glass, and top up with Coke until the mixture foams and spills onto the counter top. Quickly lick the excess off the sides of the glass and clean up the mess. If your mother catches you in the act, run for your life and blame the cat!

· ·

A Walk in the Gardens

SALENA'S MOTHER HAS SENT HER ON AN ERRAND to buy new dress material. The occasion is the wedding of a distant relative. Her mother has asked for peach satin with matching lace for herself, white for Zuhra, and Salena is allowed to choose whatever colour she wants. Salena stands for a long time fingering the various cloths before a tiny, grey-haired shop assistant asks if she needs help. Hafsa has given her precise instructions regarding the lengths required, and soon she has the correct fabric for both her mother and sister, but she finds herself incapable of choosing her own. Sky-blue or sunflower-yellow? Her mother has never allowed Salena to choose her clothes, and she finds herself incapable of making a decision. The shop assistant suggests a shade of pink and Salena agrees gratefully.

Soon she finds herself back outside the busy shop, the city booming around her with a clamour that won't go away. Her throat is parched, but she cannot get anything to drink, as Hafsa has provided her with the exact bus fare and the precise money required for the shopping. As she makes her way to the bus stop she hears her name screamed above the noise of the street. She turns in time to see Yaseen, a boy she remembers from primary school, hurrying over to her, grinning. She has a distant memory of pain associated with his name, but it is blocked out as he embraces her and the parcels she clutches to her chest. He is talking non-stop, words that stumble past her ears incomprehensibly, and she finds herself being led by the hand away from her destination towards the leafy shadows at the top of the street.

They are walking in dappled sunlight, the oak trees providing a cloak of protection against heat and noise, although she can't concentrate on his words. Salena is light-headed. No one except her baby sister has ever touched her with affection. She feels the texture of his palm, smooth and soft against the work-thickened skin of her hand. He says something that appears to require an answer and she nods, her mouth curving into the beginnings of a smile.

She sees the policeman behind Yaseen at the same moment she feels a heaviness settle on each of her shoulders, pushing her feet deeper into her shoes. At the police station she perches on a corner of a scarred brown bench, staring sightlessly down at her nails digging into her palm. The nails are too soft, they cannot penetrate the skin, and there is no comforting release of blood.

Her mother arrives to prove her identity, with Zuhra. Her little sister comes over and snuggles into her body, kitten-like, and her proximity releases the tears that Salena has held back.

Once she is home, locked into her bedroom, she takes out the seashell with its brittle sharp edge. When Hanif arrives to inflict his punishment, she is in an unreachable space.

Affinity

ZUHRA RUNS AHEAD THEN SPINS IN CIRCLES, the skirt of her turquoise-and-white checked uniform lifting to show the tops of her rounded thighs, as she waits for Salena to catch up. It is her first day at school and she can't wait to learn how to read the words in the books that have been a mystery to her for as long as she can remember. Salena has warned her that she won't be able to read at the end of the school day, that it takes time to learn the letters, but Zuhra doesn't believe her. At the classroom door Salena hands over a tiny brown school case, filled with Zuhra's favourite cheese sandwich and a bottle of orange juice. A smiling nun takes Zuhra by the hand, and she doesn't glance back at her sister.

Salena stands awkwardly for a moment, looking after her, then tiptoes lightly on the sweet-smelling passage to the door that leads to the garden. She imagines how hard it must be to clean these wooden floorboards, the effort involved in creating the perfumed shine that spreads across the ground.

Outside, she sits down on a small stone bench under a tree, the smells of summery flowers all around her. A ladybird settles on her palm, its plump red and black body belying its fragility. She cups her hands together and encloses the tiny insect in both palms, bringing her hands to her nose as though she wants to inhale its winged freedom.

An elderly nun walks by, tilts her head to the right and suggests Salena complete her prayers in the chapel, behind the bench. It takes Salena a moment to understand her accent, her words spoken in a gentle pattern, like a bedtime nursery rhyme. She makes Salena get up and waves her over to the prayer room. Salena dutifully does her bidding, releasing the ladybird onto a speckled carnation. She steps from the sunlight into the cool chapel.

The interior is tinier than Salena's bedroom, as if it were made for dolls. There is a single brown bench, its back to the door, facing a wall against which a life-size statue of a golden-haired woman stands, her lips smiling at the yellow-haired fat baby she holds tightly in both immobile arms. The baby and mother have their eyes locked together, excluding the world forever. Near the statue is a low table on which a short white candle is burning, its flame flickering like an inquisitive snake's tongue.

Salena sits down, puts her hands under her thighs, palms down, and feels the bench, wooden, warm, slightly rough. She rocks slowly, forward and backwards and, behind the statue, her watching eyes find a tiny picture, its size more suited to the room. She sees a glowing man, head bowed, arms spread, blood dripping down one cheek like tears, red drops falling from his palms. He seems unaware of the hurt, his eyes glancing away from himself. It is a look she recognises, and which she carries home with her. And though she will never enter the chapel again, that gaze lives with her until she dies.

Wedding Dress Tiers

SALENA WALKS INTO THE FRONT ROOM OF THE HOUSE carrying the tea and semolina cake which Hafsa has cut into syrupy diamonds. The three strangers are sitting on Hafsa's new rose-pink leather lounge suite, which she has bought especially for this visit. There are matching pink curtains covering the windows, which Hafsa finished sewing the night before.

When Salena walks in, her parents and their visitors, Mr and Mrs Parker and their son Zain, are talking about mutual acquaintances. Someone's second wife has run off with her stepson, who's the same age as she is. Their shocked voices don't match the half-smiles on their faces.

At Salena's appearance, the group falls silent. She pours the tea into her mother's special cups – each pink cup is gold rimmed with three gold feet and a matching gold saucer. Usually this tea set is displayed in Hafsa's glass cabinet, but today, like Salena, it has been brought out for show.

She offers a cup to Mrs Parker, who adds four teaspoons of sugar, fixing a pleasant expression on her face so that her mother cannot accuse her of being rude. She would like to look directly at the guests, especially the son, but she never raises her eyes to meet those of the people she serves, and she is scared her mother will accuse her of being forward if she looks at the man she may marry – if the Parkers like what they see.

Weeks later, her mother comes back from town with white satin and lace, and that is how Salena learns she is to be married. His parents had liked her fair skin, her parents had liked the sound of a lawyer son-in-law, and the date has been set. Her mother decides on the style of the dress – a satin bodice with Princess Anne sleeves and a skirt comprising seven frothy tiers, each succeeding tier larger than the one before.

On her wedding day, Salena vanishes into the dress, an armour of lace and satin, leaving just her face exposed to the flashes of photographer's bulbs. She remembers nothing of the day; her only reference is the huge wedding album her mother-in-law constructs to display to the endless stream of visitors. In the photographs, Salena-the-Bride sits on the huge stage in a local school hall, submerged in a sea of white, her head bowed under the weight of 22-carat gold necklaces and earrings, arms covered in bracelets. Seven bridesmaids, who are dressed in varying shades of orange, green, lilac and red, surround her.

In the first few pages of the album, she and her bridesmaids are alone on the stage, but later, after the nikah in the mosque, after the bride-price had been paid, the photographs show Zain with her on the stage. Her father has told her to ask for a hundred rand – so much money, groceries for a month – and Zain has paid it. He must really like Salena-the-Bride.

There are no photographs of her wedding night, but she has vague pictures in her head. In one such memory-photograph, Salena sees Mrs Parker, her new mother-in-law, removing Salena's dress, petticoats, jewellery, helping her into an ivory nightie. In another blurred image, she sees a stranger, a naked man, fitting a part of his body into an immobile woman. Salena herself is not there; she has slipped out of the body that naked man is penetrating. For years, her mother told her only prostitutes had sex. She cannot participate in this act.

The next morning, Mrs Parker, her new mother, comes in to change the sheets, smiling at the red stains, evidence of money well-spent.

Thirty-eight weeks later, Salena gives birth to her eldest son, Muhammad, and discovers the true purpose of sex: procreation. A year after that, almost to the day, the twins, Raqim and Makeen, are born after a protracted labour which results in a botched emergency operation, and the doctor says there may not be any more babies.

Sex becomes truly pointless, except as a means of escape into other realms. At night, when Zain pushes and prods her body, she imagines herself standing next to the bed, her arms crossed, examining the abundance of hair on his back and buttocks. Or tucked up next to the milky limbs of her sleeping sons.

Once, when Zain is particularly intent on exploring her orifices, she visualises floating all the way to London to visit her sister, just to be a breeze against Zuhra's skin as she sits on the balcony watching the crescent moon, perhaps thinking of her.

Years later, when Zain is gone, she finds her wedding album, opens it at random to a picture of herself surrounded by bridesmaids. Trapped in their photograph prison, they smile back at her like a giant bowl of colourful jellies. Salena, in the centre, is the whipped cream in this human trifle, offered up as a dessert, sold for a hundred rand.

. . . .

Trifle

1 l custard

1 Swiss roll

500 g colourful fresh fruit to taste – sliced bananas,

berries, mangos etc.

250 ml fresh cream, whipped

50 g flaked almonds

1 Cadbury's flake for garnish

Prepare the custard according to the package instructions. Allow to cool completely. (Or purchase ready-made custard.)

Slice the Swiss roll into large pieces, cut into chunks and cover the bottom of a large glass bowl with approximately one third of the roll. Add a layer of prepared fruit, then a layer of custard. Repeat the process until you are out of ingredients or the bowl is full. Top with whipped cream and garnish with almonds and chocolate.

. . . .

Of Blood and Beauty

When Father comes home, wearing that look, I know he has screwed up again and expects me to clean up after him, as usual. He says, "My dear, you know, you've always been my favourite." I wait, sniffing the red rose he has somehow acquired in the middle of winter. Another gift he pretends I've asked for. I don't like flowers. All they do is shed petals and create a mess for me to clean.

He says, "My sweet, you have the power to make me very happy or very sad."

I say nothing.

He says, "My daughter, I love you."

I remain silent.

When he believes I am suitably softened, like ice-cream forgotten in the sun, he tells me what he really wants, what it is I have to do.

After a while, I can no longer hear his words. I feel like I'm in one of those nightmares in which you find yourself trapped in a small space slowly filling with water, and you've forgotten how to swim.

But a girl must do as her father says, and the next morning I set off for the Beast's castle.

Inside, the castle is spotless, kept immaculately clean by unseen hands. You'd think this would make me happy; instead, it reminds me of the hospice where my mother was left to die. My cupboard replenishes itself with new dresses every morning. But the richness of the fabric weighs me down, making it impossible to walk, even in the soft pig's skin shoes he gives me to wear. His jewels leave faint discolourations on my wrists, and the heavy gold chains around my throat force me to speak in a strangled whisper.

His home is filled with books and mirrors. Why would a beast like him need mirrors? I do not know the woman his mirrors tell me I have become. She is gorgeous. She is without truths. So I read and I escape for hours into the only reality I have.

Still, each day the sun sets and I must trudge up the stairs to the black bedroom where he waits. He says I am his light. In the dark I see gleaming eyes worshipping me the way a sunflower follows the sun.

When he loosens my auburn hair, his claws scrape at my skull. He says I should not brush it; he wants birds to nest in it. He says my skin feels like warmed silk. I think of mulberry silkworms existing in captivity, boiled alive in their cocoons to ensure the extraction of the lengthiest strands of silk. He says he wants to clean me with his tongue. I tell him water and soap work better, but he doesn't hear me.

I find a use for the diamonds: they can cut like his raspy tongue. They can slice open layers of skin, exposing fat and muscle and sinew and the marrow in bones. There will be lumps and ridges when my skin knits together. He won't like it if I'm beastly.

Babies

EARLY MORNING, BEFORE SUNRISE, SHE HOLDS THEIR HEADS, one in each hand, as they guzzle at her breasts, making little grunts of bliss, their bodies tucked around hers. She's sitting up, propped against pillows, and she can see her older child sleeping at the bottom of the bed, like a puppy, his bottle dangling from a milk-swollen lower lip. He has kicked off his comfort-blankie and she can see goosebumps on the skin of his calves where the pants of his pyjamas have ridden up. She grasps the soft quilt that her daadi made her before she was born between the toes of her right foot and gently covers him.

The four of them have been sharing a bed since the twins' birth six months ago. Zain doesn't like the nightly squeals of feeds and nappy changes caused by the trio. They interrupt his sleep; he says the nightly disturbances are making him look haggard in the morning. He reminds her that he is the one earning money to feed all of them, so he's taken to sleeping in the bedroom at the far end of the passage.

She barely sees him anymore, except when she makes him breakfast. He insists on cooked porridge, no packets of convenient cold cereal, and eggs fried sunny-side up, the way his mother makes them. Sometimes she bumps into him when she goes to make Muhammad a bottle at two in the morning. He'll be sitting at the kitchen counter having a Coke, reading yesterday's newspaper; he might even acknowledge her with a glance. Usually she tries to hold her breath, but sometimes the odour of his earlier pursuits hangs over the kitchen like fog, impossible for her to avoid, reminding her of the cheap perfume he gave her when the twins were born. She used it once – it made the babies sneeze.

Her days are heavy with the babies. Milk feeds, then runny cereal for the twins and his father's leftover porridge for Muhammad. She bathes and dresses them individually, singing loudly to placate the others, then puts them down for a morning nap. She rinses, sterilises, washes the previous day's nappies, cleans the kitchen, gets lunch ready – pureed vegetables for the twins, fingers of fish and peas for Muhammad – and there are still the rooms to clean and Zain's supper to prepare.

Most days go by without her seeing or talking to another adult. Sometimes she wakes up from a half-doze and can't remember her name, or why she is surrounded by small bodies.

Mother's Lament

SALENA DRIVES TO THE BEACH AND LETS THE BOYS LOOSE on the blue waters. They shriek and shiver, and her eyes follow their every move, watching the drops of clear water that twinkle on their eyelashes and run down their soft skin. She remembers the sea, the beach, as a swirl of shadows, recalls singing a lullaby to Zuhra as they waited for their father's anger to subside.

She is twenty-three years old but feels middle-aged. Every day she ticks the same tasks off her imaginary list; each day is the same. Often she thinks she would welcome death with a soft sigh of relief, a deserved reward. But then she remembers the children, her anchors to this life.

Most mornings the boys wake early, demanding breakfasts of porridge and sticky fruit juice, after which they need their bums washed, their teeth brushed, their bodies covered in goblin-sized clothes. Muhammad must have his vest and underpants turned inside out, or the labels will itch him. Raqim needs his socks perfectly aligned over his little toes or his takkie will be unhappy. Makeen will not wear anything that has red in it, not even a red cotton thread, and will not wear shoes on his feet, only his hands.

Her brain manages through automatic functioning – remembers to tell the heart to beat, the lungs to inhale and exhale – but all waking and sleeping thoughts are controlled by the three boys who tug at her heart and twist her, like the dough they play with and mould into distorted animal shapes. She is their willing captive; they imprison her each night anew with their sleepy smiles.

If Salena could gaze into her future, she would choose to pause her life forever at this moment of bliss and boys, because the future holds a tragic blow.

In a few weeks' time, while Zain sleeps dreamlessly on his mother's brown leather couch, his body full of her steak and sweet yellow rice, Mrs Parker will take her much adored grandchildren into the garden. And she will leave them alone briefly as she retrieves letters from the postbox.

Little, last-born Makeen will toddle away from his brothers, pushing past the unlocked gate, and will slip into the pool, trying to reach a mysterious yellow rubber duck. His tears will mingle with the chlorinated water, and he will float to the surface like a dead leaf, waiting to be discovered by his hysterical grandmother and disbelieving father.

Salena will not accept Makeen's death. She will not believe that the warm sun continues to light the world while her boy lies under layers of damp, dark soil. She will continue to shop for three boys, throwing out Makeen's old clothes and replacing them with new garments, never to be worn. His room will become a shrine to him and a sanctuary for her. Everyone else will avoid the room; she'll spend her waking hours lying on the carpet, waiting for him to come back.

In the years ahead, Salena will dream of Makeen's last moments, hear his water-logged cries in the middle of rainy nights, and wake up to count the breaths of her living boys, until they are long grown, until they leave her house.

One day, travelling on a plane to be by Zuhra's sickbed, Salena will meet an American traveller. Deep into the dark flight, she will listen as her neighbour, his tongue loosened and made maudlin by the free liquor of South African Airways, blurts out the story of his baby's death. He will tell her of his one-hundred-and-one-day-old daughter, forgotten in the rush to get to work, entombed in his car in a strip-mall parking lot, a mere five metres from his dental offices. Salena, watching the child die in the flickering heat of the car, will listen and weep for both children. Accidents happen. She will stop blaming herself; she will realise her need to be healed.

But all this is in the future. Today, at the beach, Salena has her three boys around her, and the sun pours its rays like honey over her children, turning their yellow skins brown, brightening their smiles.

The Rescue Cat

MUHAMMAD WAKES HER UP FROM A REVERIE IN an old garden chair, where she's been sitting for an hour or more. She'd been aware of the boys playing noisily behind her in the old limbs of the loquat tree, but only notices the silence when Muhammad shakes her shoulder hard.

Raqim has climbed to the top of the tree and swung himself, like an agile monkey, onto the flat roof of the garage. There he squats, immobile, wide-eyed, looking down at her like a trapped cat. Her heart contracts painfully but she tells him calmly that she is going to get the stepladder from inside the garage and bring him down, instructing Muhammad to chat to his brother while she fetches it.

She carries the ladder outside, props it up against the garage wall, and negotiates the dozen or so steps to the edge of the roof. She motions Raqim to her and he rises, as obedient as yeasty dough. With her right hand she pulls him to her and settles his body against her hip, before retreating down the ladder in reverse, holding onto it with her left hand: a slow descent that seems to cover many miles. Back on the ground Muhammad shakes his head.

That night Salena wakes up a few minutes before the witching hour, confirming the time with a glance at the clock next to her bed. She waits. Punctually, at midnight, his screams shatter the silence. She glances over at Zain's side of the bed, undisturbed. She drags herself out of bed, her body rising along with the screams, but when she gets to his room she is too late; Muhammad is already there, climbing into his brother's bed.

She stands in the doorway, watches her eldest son cover Raqim with the duvet, pat his brother's back, whisper words into his ear. She feels a lump in her throat; she wishes she could be consoled like that. As abruptly as he wakes up, Raqim goes back to sleep. Still, she waits until both boys' breathing becomes regular before leaving.

Back in her own bed she hugs a pillow to her body, aware that she won't be able to sleep for a while. Raqim's nightmares began three years ago, shortly after Makeen's death. Night after night he wakes up bewildered and howling, a lost puppy. Sometimes she gets there before Muhammad and holds Makeen, rocking him back to sleep, slowly silencing his pain. Some nights he will only accept reassurances from Muhammad. Zuhra has suggested she get Raqim a cat, something warm and furry and alive to cuddle at night.

The next day Salena takes the boys to the local animal shelter where they tell the woman in charge to choose a kitten on their behalf. She brings in a tattered black beast, with half a sagging tail. He'd been dumped from a moving car on the nearby freeway and brought in to the shelter by a driver who had witnessed the incident. Raqim reaches for him, murmuring into his raggedy fur. Peanut Butter. They become inseparable and, after a few weeks, night-time in their house is peaceful, only interrupted by Zain's clumsy early-morning returns.

Dishwashing Daydreams

THE EARLY MORNING WINTER LIGHT CLIMBS THROUGH the kitchen blinds to play in the soapy water. Salena is at the sink, washing the serving dishes in preparation for Zain's guests. She gazes up occasionally at her reflection in the kitchen window, milky with raindrops.

It's Ramadan, and Zain has invited three of his colleagues and their families to eat at their house. Salena can't decide what to make as a main meal, but her sons have inappropriately suggested gingerbread boys for dessert. She decides to phone Zuhra for some suggestions. Her sister tells her she's an idiot to be wasting her cooking skills on people she doesn't know or care about. Zuhra, her first semester of university behind her, proposes that Zain is a chauvinistic moron and that Salena should insist that he take them all out for supper.

She hasn't used this crockery set in years, not since Makeen's death. She wipes away the excess dust before immersing each dish in the water, wishing it were so easy to wash away her memories. If only she could make a gingerbread Makeen-boy and breathe life into him.

Behind her, at the breakfast nook, the boys are eating porridge with the rapidity and relish of growing bodies. She turns and catches Muhammad licking his snout joyfully. Raqim offers up a bowl, cleaned of all food debris, ready, he says, to be returned to the kitchen cupboard.

Salena still cannot believe, five years after Makeen's death, that life continues to surge ahead. Each day, when she looks at Raqim, she imagines the stark contrast between this breathing boy and his replica, now skeleton and teeth, in his small, once-white shroud. There are days when Makeen's absence weighs heavily on her. Without the boys' incessant chatter and demands, she doubts she would ever get out of bed.

She stares out the window that she cleaned the previous day with newspapers and methylated spirits, watches the rain run off the glass, and falls into her favourite reverie, the one in which she has three sons.

In her dream it is late at night. Her three sons are asleep in their beds, while outside, beyond the safety of the house and garden, cars splash through puddles of rising water. Lightning bolts brighten the sky like fireworks during Diwali. Salena is alone in the kitchen – Zain is still at the office, working late, as usual.

In her imagination it is not the phone that transmits the news, the way it did when Makeen died. Instead, the doorbell rings, and at the door are two policemen. *I'm sorry, your husband has died in a car crash.* And she cries, but not too much; her mascara does not leave black streaks on her cheeks.

The rain stops, a little sunlight shines through the window. It is not midnight, and behind her there are only two boys, and Zain is still breathing, somewhere, with someone else.

....

Burfi

500 g Nestlé powdered milk

1 can Nestlé cream

250 g icing sugar

1 tsp powdered elachi

1 cup water

1 cup sugar

5 ml rose water

½ cup ground almonds

Mix the powdered milk and cream in a food processor until it resembles fine bread crumbs. Add the icing sugar and elachi to the mixture and stir well. Boil the sugar, water and rose syrup until it thickens. Remove from heat and stir into the powdered milk mixture. Add the ground almonds, and mix again. Pour into a square serving dish and refrigerate for 3 hours or until set. Cut into squares. You could decorate these with slivered, tinted almonds. A heavenly sweet that should be shared only with true dessert lovers.

. . . .

Sunday Lunch

SALENA IS COOKING LUNCH, VEGETABLE CURRY FOR ZUHRA and chicken curry for everyone else. Zuhra has promised to make a trifle. Salena smiles, imagining the excessively polite way her sister will offer Zain a bowl of the dessert. Zuhra will tell him it's good for him, filled with nuts; brain food. He'll smile his thanks, oblivious to the insult, and Zuhra will exchange looks with Salena and wink. Salena remembers a time when a young Zuhra spent weeks in front of the mirror teaching herself to wink, and long hours practising snapping her thumb and middle finger together until she heard the satisfying click. Now her sister is all grown up, already in her second year at university.

Salena pulls on yellow kitchen gloves, then places the whole headless chicken on the draining board and expertly opens its body with a single sharp slice of the knife, exposing its entrails. Each time she cleans a chicken she feels like a pathologist working on the body of a baby, examining the fragile soft tissue and yielding bone. But today she won't think about Makeen. She scoops out the fowl's innards, removes the fatty skin that the boys won't eat, chops the remains into portions, rinses the blood off the flesh and adds it to the simmering pot.

She removes her gloves, throws them in the sink and then washes her hands with dishwashing liquid and steaming water. Her left palm tingles for a brief moment and she holds it up to the gleaming tap and notices a new incision. She can't remember making that cut. She looks at the tiny crusty scars on her hand that no one has ever noticed except Zuhra. She's told her sister it's a type of eczema that doesn't respond to treatment. She can't explain to Zuhra that a hunger inside of her compels her some days to make nicks in her palms. Would Zuhra believe she doesn't feel the pain, but that the sight of the blood confirms she is not dead? Of course Zuhra would want to know why Salena does this to herself, and Salena cannot answer that question.

The vegetable curry – brinjal, butternut, broccoli, green peppers, mushrooms, carrots and two fat red chillies – is ready, and she garnishes it with heaps of dhania the way Zuhra likes it, remembers to add curry leaves to the cooking chicken and stirs the bubbling rice. The boys run into the kitchen, shouting their joy; her mother and sister have arrived and she smiles back at them, wondering if there will be enough leftovers for supper or if she should bake a loaf of brown bread for a light evening meal.

After the Awakening

It wasn't the kiss that woke me. It was simple coincidence that he arrived at the same time the spell splintered, a century later. That's why the thorns proved trifling, as immaterial as shadows; that's why they parted for him.

He thinks he's special. He thinks he rescued me from a dreamless slumber. Actually, I had a vivid dream life: serialised dreams that couldn't compare to his dull reality (What colour scheme should we have at the nuptials? A chocolate cake or a traditional fruit one?). He is not the man of my dreams. He refuses to understand that I would rather have one of the princes who were pierced to death by the thorns; a rotting corpse would be preferable to him.

He wears a smug smile when he tells people: "I woke her up, it was my kiss that did it!" I tell him I would have preferred an electric tooth-brush and a cinnamon cappuccino. He thinks I'm joking. He seems to think I should be grateful. He acts as though I am a fridge, closed and dark, only lighting up when he opens the door.

He thinks I long for sleep because it is familiar. He says I will learn to crave him the way he does me. But I would rather sleep than listen to him recount for the millionth time how those thorns parted for him. So I snooze before breakfast, have a siesta after lunch, a catnap during dinner and the whole forty winks when he practises his lovemaking act on me. Dull, dull, dull. With him around, sleep is my choicest lover.

He brings me neat white oval pills and says, "Take these, they'll help you stay awake." I pretend to swallow while secreting them under the exquisitely embroidered pillow which has been my best friend for ten decades. He has no idea who I am. Sleep is infinitely more seductive than watching him, night after excruciatingly tedious night, examining his reflection for imperfections. He is blind to his biggest deficiency, incarcerated in his head. He thinks he's Prince Charming (who, incidentally, has to be Muslim – he's married to Snow White, Sleeping Beauty and Cinderella). I suggest to him that he's not my true love. He dismisses my thoughts with a wave of his manicured nails and chooses our garments for the wedding.

I doze through most of the reception, waking up in time for the toast. I hand him the golden goblet with its powdered surprise. I have prepared it with the same care I take to ready my body for sleep each night. He smiles at me before he gulps the liquid. I stretch my lips in response.

Then he places the back of his hand on his forehead in a poignant display of femininity before he collapses in a swoon. I hear the satisfying thunk his head makes on the inflexible floor. The idiot. He never understood that he was a mere boy, while I am a woman who's lived for a hundred and sixteen years.

Recorder Blues

SALENA IS UP IN THE DARK HOURS OF THE MORNING, before the birds start their relentless singing. She gets breakfast ready, packs school bags, checks homework again; she particularly enjoys geometry, with its precise angles and calming theorems.

Salena obsesses about her children's homework. They don't understand that while mommy is helping them, she is teaching herself. She lives in dread of her boys discovering that she never went to high school. Often she feels shaky, discussing things with her sons that she has learnt about in their own textbooks only the night before, while they lay sleeping.

Geometry, trigonometry, history and science, she absorbs like a sponge, spending the better part of her day studying, reading, researching.

At night, when Zain has sex with her, she closes her eyes and re-reads pages from textbooks as they float across the back of her eyelids. If she has been studying biology, she imagines herself as a giant praying mantis chomping off Zain's head to speed up the ejaculation procedure. She walks away, her eggs fertilised, the now useless Zain still moving his body rhythmically while she chews his head to a pulp. Sometimes she is the queen bee, mating high in the sky. Zain's penis breaks off inside her, his drone's job done, and he falls from the sky to the ground, dead.

When Muhammad finishes Standard Six, she is proud and horrified to think that on paper he is more educated than her. The boys come home from school with As for history essays and gold stars for compositions, homework she has assisted with, and Salena feels validated. But she cannot imagine enrolling herself in night school; she is filled with both shame and lethargy.

Salena does all the household chores, cooking, cleaning, laundering, polishing. By 10 am the house is spotlessly clean, lunch has been made and the supper planned, perhaps even cooked, if Zain is having guests over. She spends the rest of the morning doing research for her son's homework projects.

One Monday Salena finds Muhammad's recorder lying on his bed. Without a thought, she slips it between her lips. The tinny, whistling sound makes her smile. An hour later, she has figured out how to play "Hot Cross Buns" by following the photographic instructions in his music textbook.

During the course of the term, on the days when Muhammad does not have recorder lessons, Salena teaches herself to play more tunes, and learns how to pinch out the E # with her thumb so that it doesn't sound blurred or squeaky.

After a few weeks, Salena starts making up her own short pieces of music. Listening to the purity of the notes, she feels the air in her lungs being expelled, moving forward as sweet, delicate notes.

On the morning of Raqim's thirteenth birthday, she sends him off to school with a home-baked chocolate cake and comes back to clean out Makeen's room, to throw away the toys that have been waiting for his return for a decade.

Hot Cross Buns for the Recorder

Birds in Flight

SALENA IS SITTING IN THE MIDDLE SEAT, between her two boys, her feet resting on a soft blue overnight bag. They are on their way to England to attend Zuhra's wedding. She can't believe her baby sister is old enough to be getting married. She can't imagine the man Zuhra has chosen to marry. She can't imagine Zuhra married.

Zuhra has told her that the nikah will be at Aunty Anjum's house instead of a mosque, as she wants to be present during the ceremony. Salena thinks of her own wedding conducted in a mosque between her father and Zain and the male witnesses. Perhaps Zain never married her; perhaps he's been married to her father all these years.

An hour into the flight Raqim, sitting on her left, is still fidgeting. He pulls down the food tray in front of him and then snaps it shut forcefully several times until the man in the seat ahead turns around to glare at him. He opens and closes his seatbelt a few dozen times, with loud metallic clicks. Then he tilts his chair into a reclining position before moving it upright forcefully, once, twice, thrice. When he attempts to do it a fourth time Salena puts a restraining hand on him and offers him a banana which he accepts, unpeels and pushes into his mouth in a single motion. It is hard to believe that he is a fifteen-year-old human. He is as edgy as Peanut Butter on the way to the vet.

On her right, Muhammad is absorbed in a book on inventions, *From Abacus to Zip*. She offers him a pear, he smiles, thanks her, examines it from several perspectives for blemishes, wipes it on the front of his green T-shirt and then nips gently at the yellow skin, as though afraid of hurting the fruit. He settles deeper into his seat with a soft sigh and goes back to his book.

Raqim has discovered the button that brings flight attendants to his side. First water, then Coke, then milk. Eventually Salena intervenes with a look of silent distress that forces him to settle down and read his book: a graphic novel about a wild horse living on the prairies of North America.

Salena moves her seat back and relaxes, finally. She is glad that neither Zain, who says he has to work, nor her mother, who is recovering from a minor operation, is attending the wedding. She is free from their restrictions and demands. She imagines this is how birds in flight must feel.

The Middle Boy

There was once a second son, Luke, who despaired of his position in the centre of a trio of boys. He felt constricted as son number two; he did not have the status of his firstborn brother, Adam, nor was he the spoilt darling of the family like his baby brother Joel. He was aware that his despondency was called middle-child syndrome, but this did not make him feel any better. When Adam left to study in a far-off land, Luke wished it was his younger brother who was leaving. He was jealous of the way their mother looked at Joel with tender eyes, while he seemed to be transparent.

One day a terrible accident befell the baby brother and he died. Luke, who had yearned for his brother's absence, was guilty and grief-stricken; months later he still mourned his brother and watched helplessly his mother's slow decline into depression at the absence of her precious baby.

A year after his brother's death he told his mother he was leaving home to seek his fortune. She seemed not to hear him, but at his departure she gave him some food and the half-grown kitten that had been born to the family cat some months before. It was a brown tabby, covered in black satiny swirls, with a perfect M marked on its forehead as though drawn by a master calligrapher.

The first night away Luke shared his food with the cat before making a bed for himself under a leafy oak tree, while the cat curled up in a branch overhead. It was a balmy spring night and soon the boy dozed off into a dreamless sleep, only to be rudely awoken by the piping voice of his dead baby brother coming from above his head. But it was the cat, talking in its sleep. Luke's cries awoke the mammal, who at first pretended ignorance before admitting that he was Joel, Luke's younger brother, reborn in the form of a cat. Luke was delighted and clasped the cat to his chest joyfully. He wanted to return to their mother immediately but his baby brother said it was unlikely she would want a cat replacement for the child she missed so dreadfully.

When morning came they continued their journey. Very soon Luke ran out of food, and had it not been for Joel's hunting abilities, they would have starved. Weeks went by, Luke lost his puppy fat on the high-protein diet, and the daily hike defined his youthful muscles. Still, his search for work proved fruitless.

It was almost the end of summer when the brothers arrived at a popular riverside picnic spot, where several people were enjoying the last of the warm weather. Luke noticed a beautiful young woman look him up and down disdainfully before turning away from him to join an elegant group of well-dressed people. She'd made him acutely aware of how unkempt he was: his elbows and knees poked out of the holes in his clothes, which were threadbare and too small for him. His cat-brother caught a couple of ducks for their lunch, and after eating their fill the boys rested on the banks of the rushing river.

The warm, dozy air was suddenly filled with loud cries for help coming from the middle of the river. The brothers jumped up and saw a man in obvious difficulty in the river's centre. Luke turned to Joel, who shook his head. He was a cat; water was the enemy. Luke briefly looked around at the other people gathered near the river. No one seemed eager to jump into the flowing waters, so it was up to him. He dove in and swam with his smooth young muscles and heaved the bedraggled man to the shallow lip of the river. The onlookers woke up as if from a mass trance, and hands helped him and the near-fatality out of the water.

The swimmer and Luke were quickly helped out of their sodden clothes and provided with warm clothing, the richness of which Luke, accustomed to Adam's hand-me-downs, had never known before. The same girl who had snubbed him earlier approached him and gushed her thanks for saving her father, a noted conjurer, while openly admiring the way his new attire moulded itself to his body.

Her father approached and offered his daughter's hand to Luke as a reward for his lifeguard duties. But Luke remembered the way she had looked at him when he was shabbily dressed and declined the offer. Instead, he told the magician that all he wished for was for his cat-brother to be human again. Hardly had the words left his mouth when Joel stepped out of a puff of black smoke, human again, looking like his twin.

The magician also provided them with a huge bag of gold, and they returned to their mother, in a snazzy silver BMW. When the mother saw her sons she wept for joy. She was healed. Soon the older brother returned from his studies and the reunited family lived together happily, Luke secure in the magician's parting words: "The middle child is the heart of the family."

Love, Unconditional

IT'S THREE O'CLOCK IN THE MORNING, ALMOST DAWN OR, depending on your viewpoint, the darkest time of night. For Salena it is a time of ghosts and shadows. She sits, sleepless, in Raqim's room, praying, making deals with Allah for his safe return. When he was little, all she wanted was for him to grow up, to change, so that he would no longer remind her of his dead twin. Now Salena would give anything to return him to the safety of childhood, before the onset of these teenage years which have turned him into a stranger who steals from her to answer the chemical cries of his body.

All she wants is for him to be sleeping safely in his bed, so her imagination and body can rest. Instead, she waits, paces, watches from the window out of which he has slipped.

In the morning, she will phone a security company to install burglar bars and an alarm system. The window will not be his escape route again. Peanut Butter glides into the room, purring, looking for an owner who no longer cares about him. It has fallen to Salena to caress and feed the once-adored pet.

She has watched her precious but cranky son, the older twin by two minutes, go from being an outgoing, imaginative soul to an inward-looking monster, intent on his next fix. Salena has tried everything to help him, to no avail.

Zain's response is to beat him, and when she intervenes, flash-backs to her own childhood almost blinding her, he blames her for being too soft a mother. He says if she won't let him hit the child, she should sort it out herself; he will no longer help.

Another hour has vanished, and still there is no sign of him. Salena does blame herself, and the burden of the blame gives her a permanent backache that will not go away, despite painkillers and medical intervention. Maybe after Makeen's death she should have spent more time with the boys instead of withdrawing into her own sorrow.

She goes downstairs and makes another pot of coffee, opens the fridge, looking for something to eat. She decides on dhania chutney and toast. While she eats, she reads the Classified section of the newspaper Zain has left lying in the kitchen. Her eye falls on the obituaries, and she recalls her obsession with reading this column after Makeen's drowning. For almost a year, she went to the funerals of children she found in the column. She would hug the blank mothers and then cry all the way home.

That day, in a rare moment of synchronicity, she sees an advertisement at the end of the Deaths column. A Christian-based drug rehabilitation centre on a farm in the Eastern Cape. She considers the cost of his possible recovery. If he should find Christianity but abandon drugs, it is a price she is willing to pay in gold. She sips at her coffee, sees Peanut Butter raise his face to the ceiling, and hears the thud almost immediately. Her son is home. It is precisely 4 am when she dials the centre's number, but the voice that answers does not express impatience, only a tired helpfulness.

When she goes up to his room, he is asleep, or pretending to be asleep. Either way, he does not stir as she packs the bare minimum of his clothes and personal necessities. At 5 am, a car from the local branch of the rehab centre arrives for him. She lets two burly men into the house and shows them his room. They escort him downstairs; he wears the frightened face of the three-year-old who buried his twin. He begs, he pleads, but the part of her heart that belongs to him has turned to ice. She turns away from his sobs, without a backward glance, carrying Peanut Butter into bed with her. And she does not visit him while he is away, even when they tell her she can.

Salena doesn't know what happens to him in those two years he's gone. She thinks of him daily, but refuses to contact him. She lets go of him, as she was forced to let go of his twin.

Seven hundred and forty two days later he is home, whole and healed, proudly displaying his matric certificate, a computer-course diploma, his blood-test results, and a horse-riding medal.

But it is only after a further two years of clean blood tests that she stops searching his room, that she grows complacent with the milk and bread money. And only when he is awarded a scholarship by a local university does she allow her heart to melt, just a little.

....

Prayer for a Loved One in Need

1 white candle

matches

Very early, on the first morning after a new moon, find a quiet space and light a white candle of any shape or size. Observe the flame for a while until it burns steadily, with as few flickers as possible. When you are absolutely tranquil, visualise the person you love, who requires a fortification of his inner strength or who needs to abandon self-destructive behaviour.

Picture your loved one surrounded by rays of light and love. Conjure up a perfect place for this person in the near future, at the end of the current period of upset in his life, where you can see him as whole, healthy and healed. Then find a warm place in your heart for him, and keep him safe.

Repeat this process for three mornings over a period of three new moons. But remember, if he is not ready to accept help, you cannot waste your energies on him. You need to be prepared to move on, and leave him until he's ready.

....

Nazma

SALENA IS ALLOWED TO VIEW THE BABY FOR A FEW minutes when she is pushed in her incubator, up to the glass window of the neonatal intensive-care unit. Her sucking reflex is undeveloped, so she is being fed her mother's expressed breast milk through piping that is affixed to her nostril. Salena would like to cuddle her, but not even Zuhra can do that. Her mother has to touch her through the openings on either side of the incubator.

The pink and white card attached to the inside of her incubator informs anyone who can read that Nazma weighed a mere one thousand and twenty grams at birth, and both Apgar tests were recorded as one out of ten. When Zuhra first sees this she moans and says to Salena that failing your first test can't bode well for an academic life. As soon as the baby escapes the incubator, she's burning the identification card so that Nazma never sees evidence of her stupidity. Jimmy tells her that according to the baby magazines he reads, the tests are not indicative of intelligence; they are simply to assess the baby's health. Zuhra shudders at the mention of the baby magazines she despises and shakes her head mournfully.

Zuhra and Jimmy come to stand next to Salena and they watch the tiny being sleeping, her hands in fists on either side of her head. Her only piece of clothing, aside from a disposable nappy that reaches up to her minute nipples, is a woolly white hat from which a dark curl escapes. Her left arm is taped in white bandage, like a mini-cast, and medication is pumped through its wrappings into her almost invisible veins. Salena tells Zuhra that Nazma looks like a microscopic angel, and Jimmy nods his agreement. Zuhra suggests that they have their eyes tested. She says the child looks like a newborn rat, minus the tail. But she smiles and says she can learn to feel fondly about rats. Then she goes off to express milk, as she has been doing every three or four hours since Nazma's birth.

Salena and Jimmy watch the baby for a while longer. Neither can shake off the baby-rat image. They go downstairs to the hospital's coffee shop, and Jimmy leaves Salena alone for a minute to fetch something from his car. He returns with three bags of clothes for premature babies.

Salena drinks two cups of coffee and eats a slice of too-rich chocolate cake while Jimmy unpacks each item of fairy-sized clothing and explains their purpose to her. She thinks of Zain's complete indifference to the birth of his children; he never went shopping for them, never changed a nappy and never asked her how she coped with three children under two years. Her sons have grown up like the children of a single mother. Zuhra says perhaps that is why they have turned out so well: Muhammad studying medicine, much to Hafsa's delight, and Raqim finishing his degree in science with the idea of studying veterinary science abroad – to his grandmother's bewilderment. Salena is often overwhelmed by her love and gratitude for them.

Zuhra finds her husband and sister drinking coffee under a heap of miniature garments, and she smiles tiredly at Jimmy as he draws her close to him. Salena, watching them from across the table, experiences a moment of heartbreak.

A Mother's Love

There was once a woman who performed a magic spell to have the daughter of her longings, of her dreams. When the baby was born, she was tiny like a rosebud, ethereal as a whiff of candle smoke. The mother was horrified by her child's fragility, and blamed herself for not wording the spell correctly. Nevertheless, she loved the little girl immediately and intensely, and cared for her tirelessly.

One day, when the mother woke up, she found her child had been snatched out of her shoe-box crib by the toad that lived in the woman's back garden. The same toad the woman had fed through the winter with heaps of buttered white bread. "Talk about biting the hand that feeds you," muttered the woman to herself as she marched down to the lake that bordered their house and demanded the toad show her face.

"I'm sorry," said Mother Toad, "but your daughter's really pretty, and I want my son to marry someone beautiful instead of a relative. I want good-looking grandchildren!"

"So you kidnapped her? How dare you! Where is my child?"

Mother Toad hung her head and explained that the girl had been rescued by a fish and a butterfly from her lily-pad prison, and had escaped before the wedding ceremony could take place.

The woman had always been kind to animals before, caring for them, not eating their flesh, not even wearing their skins, but now she discovered a brutality in her character of which she'd been unaware; it was the fierceness of her maternal love. She placed her inelegant bare heel on the toad's back and crushed the creature under her foot, hardly noticing the oozing slime that squelched beneath her sole as she strode off on her quest to find her daughter.

She began by interrogating the insects. Then she found a field mouse that had provided her daughter with shelter in exchange for housework and agreeing to marry the mouse's neighbour, an elderly blind mole. The second arranged marriage proposition her poor child had had to endure. Mrs Mouse said a sick swallow had flown off with the girl before the wedding. The mother was livid on her daughter's behalf. She made short work of Mrs Mouse and Mr Mole; they were soon in greener pastures. But still she could not find her daughter.

She hired a private investigator, she visited a psychic, she approached the media for help, but to no avail. Then one day the mother heard a knock on her front door, a rat-tat-tat that she recognised instantly. She rushed to the door and there stood her baby, her daughter, still small, but all grown up, with wings, and as lovely as ever.

"Mom," she cried, and enveloped her mother in a hug as strong as a bear. Then she recounted her adventures, from the moment the toad (her mother had long ago got the exterminator in, and all the toads on the property had gone to watery graves) had stolen her from her mother's side to her escape from the mole and the mouse (moles had been bombed underground, mice had been trapped) on the back of a kind swallow she'd nursed back to health. The mother decided not to mention the spell she'd been developing to ground and mute birds forever.

Then she shyly showed her mother a sparkling ring of hardened nectar. "My prince," she said, "of the Blossoms. My choice; my own kind. I met him in a flower, and we've spent a lot of time getting to know each other. He's given me wings as a pre-nuptial gift: I can fly close to the sun, I can feel its rays on my back, the infinite blue sky is my playground. I am small, but no longer locked."

The mother was silent. Then she said, "Well, if you're sure you're happy, I'll learn to tolerate a son-in-law."

The Mirror Cracks

ONE MORNING, SOME MONTHS AFTER RETURNING from a prolonged visit to Zuhra, who was recovering from a breast cancer scare, Salena wakes up realising that what she feels towards Zain is more than spousal animosity: she truly despises him. She is sick of hearing how she doesn't contribute to the household financially, how every possession belongs to him, and worn out by all the years of cleaning up after him.

For the first time in their married lives, they are the only people in the house. The years she has spent guiding her sons through school have paid off, although Zain does not consider her mothering worthy of the title "labour". Muhammad has completed his medical studies but has decided to take a year off to travel before deciding which field to specialise in, and Raqim is fulfilling his dream of becoming a vet, studying at an American university full-time and working part-time to supplement his financial support.

She and Zain are alone in a five-bedroom, six-bathroom house, unless you count the TVs that Zain collects as living entities. They embody most rooms with their non-stop chattering channels.

She notices the three towels he scatters on the bathroom floor like empty sweet wrappers. She sees his socks forsaken in piteous piles. One pair at the bottom of the stairs, another pair in front of the lounge TV; once, incongruously, a single, smelly sock next to the stove.

In the morning, evidence of his bedtime snacks are lying on the floor next to his side of the bed. The curl of a naartjie peel. A packet of Marie biscuits with just one biscuit left. A half-empty bottle of juice.

In his study, his jeans lie discarded on the floor, the shape of his bum still stamped on them.

She observes.

At night, in bed, while she reads, he cleans his nose, rubbing the snot between thumb and index finger before bouncing it onto the wooden floors.

She watches.

In the mornings, she sees the devastation in the kitchen. He has left five dirty glasses from the night before, with remnants of Coke or juice still in them. Then various breakfast plates, a coffee mug, un-eaten toast. He leaves a trail of crumbs and used cutlery from kitchen to dining room to lounge to bathroom, to bed.

That night, when he arrives home, he pours a glass of water, sips at it, discards the glass. Then he reaches for another glass, fills it with juice, and leaves the juice carton next to the sink. At the table, he pours a third glass, Coke, to accompany his meal.

He burrows into the plate with his right hand, food marinating his fingers to the uppermost knuckles, sauce saturating his chin, re-minding her of Faruk's table manners. In the middle of eating, he rises from the table, carrying puris and a chicken leg to the television, dripping food along the way, unperturbed.

She goes to bed.

The next morning, she hears from the en-suite bathroom the sound of him emptying his bowels, trumpeting out farts. Followed by the sounds of throat-clearing, gurgles and gargles in the shower. When Zain has left for work, Salena draws the curtains against the sunlight and spends the day in bed.

In the evening, he walks around his unspoilt domestic carnage, oblivious. She stands, casually clearing a space on the kitchen coun-ter, shattering the soiled crockery on the floor. He grunts something at her from his space in front of a TV screen, but does not get up to see what has happened.

Salena crunches her way with bare skin over the shards, and walks upstairs to their bedroom. There are bits of crockery embedded in her feet, and she leaves a trail of blood. At the doorway, she catches her eye in the full-length mirror which is positioned against the far wall of the bedroom. Automatically, she straightens her shoulders, lifts up her neck, smoothes her hair. In front of the mirror, she lifts up her eyebrows to make her eyes widen and pulls back the skin at the outer corners of her eyes, narrows her nose and sucks in her cheeks slightly. She's in her forties; there's no stopping the ageing process now, unless she wants to indulge in cosmetic surgery.

In the mirror's Mr Minned surface, she sees at least two possible futures for herself. In one, she has become her Aunt Polla, bitter and jealous and perpetually blaming others for her own wretchedness. In another, she sees red lights, brown boulders and metallic debris, molten glass – a terrifying scene, yet tempting.

Then, for the briefest second, she catches a glimpse of her beloved daadi in the mirror, and it gives her power. The mirror cracks, then shatters completely. Shards are flying around the room, but she closes her eyes, feels herself in her grandmother's protective embrace. Peace envelops her.

After an interminable time, a whimper pierces her calm. She turns to face the sound, leaving a bloody shadow behind her, and sees Zain poised in the doorway, a shard of mirror trapped in his neck.

Reflections

I know what they whisper behind my back, I've seen their smirks: She used to tidy up after seven men before Prince Charming married her. Don't they appreciate that cleanliness is next to godliness? Not one of them would know how to purify a pig-sty of a cottage let alone disinfect a dilapidated castle. Am I a domestic slave? Perhaps. But I'm not going to publicise the fact like Cinderella, self-condemned to cleaning up after others for eternity. I've got bigger issues.

Today, in the shadowy hours of the morning, as the enchanting mirror and I were adoring each other, I saw it. An ominous phantom, priming my snowy skin for its coal-lump future. It was nesting, near the outer corner of my right eyelid, like a viper. A hostile wrinkle casting a sickening shadow on the mirror's satiny surface.

A howl escaped my red-as-blood lips, and the mirror sobbed its cold-comfort response, knowing I was forever changed; a crone in creation.

I have no one to turn to. At the wedding reception, the prince made my mother dance to her death in red-hot iron shoes. Mommy knew me best of all; Mommy loved me. She tried to murder me several times because she understood I could never endure the horror of maturing like a mould-ripened piece of brie, the way she had.

The prince admires my smooth flawlessness. He doesn't want me resembling creased foil; he requires a stunning statue. At night when he slobbers over my body, he says, "Darling, don't move, don't breathe!" I have to pretend to sleep. It's not that I mind indulging his necrophilic fantasies; I was at my happiest preserved in that magnificent glass casket, relentlessly beautiful, perpetually young. But then he came along and fell in love with my motionless shape. If only the dwarves had refused him, if only they hadn't tripped while carrying my coffin, if only I hadn't coughed up Mommy's kind-heartedly poisoned lump of apple. If only I could stop the ghastly progression of time.

The path forward is a slick tilt into old age, a second-by-second descent into unsightliness. At least I have no one to protect: I don't have a daughter who needs me to rescue her. I have only myself to think of.

High Care

"I'M IN HIGH CARE," THE STRANGE MAN SAYS, unprovoked. He smiles, showing fleshy red gums, his head tilted right, his eyes shining.

"That's … nice," Salena replies.

"Yes, it is. Here, we have special days for high-care patients. Which section are you in?"

"I'm, er, not sure."

"Ah, so you'll be waiting for your interview then."

"Yes, I suppose …"

Salena walks away from him briskly, opening the patio doors that lead into the back garden with its broad view of the mountain.

As she strolls around the sanatorium's grounds, Salena remembers Zuhra's humid garden and the grave she'd dug to bury the mink coat. She remembers hearing the call of the lonely alligator from the nearby Everglades; it had seemed to echo the cry that lived in her own body. When Zuhra had gone inside to eat, she'd stayed behind to listen for the alligator. But it had never called out again.

When she got better, Zuhra said she and Salena should go on a road trip, but Salena declined. She'd spent enough time in the US. Besides, driving made her think of cops: on their first day out, with Zuhra at the wheel, they were stopped by a burly Floridian police officer. A routine driving licence check, he said, but Salena was reminded of the Afrikaner policemen of her youth.

In her dreams, Salena could still feel their thick red fingers on her arms, like iron bracelets, as the inquisitive eyes of a squirrel watched her from a low branch. The police had asked if she and Yaseen had

had sex. One had said he would put his fingers up Salena to see if she was wet, to see if she was a virgin.

Salena had pleaded, "I'm not white, I'm not white!" But they wouldn't believe her. Then Ma had arrived, with her Indian card, and she'd known it would be worse for her at home.

In the garden, she lights the menthols she's stolen off the front desk. She's never smoked before, and she splutters like an old car as she inhales. She can imagine Zuhra telling her to extinguish the cigarette on Zain's eyeball, or some other ball, but instead she stubs it out on the base of her lifeline and watches impassively as the skin darkens and shrivels. Soon there will be a new scar to join the others.

She thinks, this is not her life, this is a role to which she's forgotten the lines, and if she looks around suddenly, she will catch the audience, watching her, laughing at her. Zain says she needs help, that she is sick, she tried to kill him. She doesn't argue. She can't remember. Maybe she *did* try to kill him. Maybe she *is* sick.

She remembers her conversation with Dr Galsband earlier that day. He's convinced she meant to murder Zain. He said that if Salena had succeeded in killing Zain, she would have died, too. Perhaps not physically, but she would have been imprisoned by that act forever, a kind of death.

"Like my marriage," said Salena.

"Would it have been worth it?"

"Yes," said Salena. "If only for the order and cleanliness left behind by his death. But, you know, I don't believe I tried to kill him. Maybe I was trying to kill myself."

Dr Galsband was not impressed with her answer.

It is he who has made Salena come outside with a pencil and paper, to sit on the bench under the oak tree in the back garden and write a list of things she would miss if she were dead.

Salena takes a bite out of the apple crumble she has saved from lunch. It is the only thing that looked edible. Then, ever-obedient, she follows the doctor's orders.

Ten things I would miss if I were dead

1. I would miss the smell of percolated coffee in the morning.
2. I would miss sleeping.
3. I would miss my sister and my sons.

She chews at the end of her pencil. There is a burst of wind through the garden, and a few crunchy leaves land on the bench next to her, clearing a space from the tree and her mind. She thinks of how good she has always been. How obedient, like a cow chewing her way to the slaughterhouse. Succumbing to her parents' rules and regulations, her mother's worry about what people would think. Submitting meekly to Zain – after all, he earned the money, and all she did was give birth to babies and cook and clean his house and have sex with him on demand. Never questioning his rights over her, crawling back into her body and living through her sons.

The nurse opens the patio door, beckons to her. But Salena shakes her head. Not yet. She is not quite ready. She can't think of any more points to add to the list, but there is something else she needs to write before she can face Dr Galsband and his interrogations again. A letter.

I see you in the faces of other children as you flit by in pursuit of your childish goals. I am despondent; I can never hold you, never make eye-contact with you as we share a joke, and never see you smile at me sleepily as I tuck you into bed at night.

You will not have to face the anguish of adolescence. You will never taste a first kiss.

We will never go shopping for your first suit. We will not discuss women. Or men. I will not be able to complain about your brothers' taste in music; you will not roll your eyes at my maudlin musical choices when I drive you to school. You will never go to school.

Your tongue will never again taste my pancakes made sweet with sugar, fragrant with cinnamon and tangy with the juice of a fresh lemon.

Your eyes will not catch mine during a poetry reading, when the words jump from the voice of the poet into your heart.

We will not walk together on the beach, sand stuck in our underwear and toes. We will not jump up together to dance to the melodic beat of "our" song.

Of course, you will never have to compromise. You will never have to worry about being too fat or too thin or not rich enough. You will never be hurt. You will never know fear. You will never be sad. You will never stub your toe. You will never break your heart.

You will not be lonely. You will never have to swallow your pride. You will not fail. You will never lie. You will never be late for a plane. You will never commit a crime. You will not doubt yourself. You will never face sorrow which leaves you too frozen to breathe. You will not hold my hand when I die.

I miss you every day.

All my love
Your mother

....

Gingerbread Boys

125 g butter

2 tbsp golden syrup

¾ cup sugar

1 egg, beaten

2 cups self-raising flour, sifted

¼ tsp salt

2 tsp ground ginger

½ tsp cinnamon

½ tsp ground cloves

Lightly cover a baking tray with non-stick spray. Melt the butter and golden syrup in a pot, then add the sugar and the egg. Lastly, add the flour, salt, ginger, cinnamon and cloves, and mix well.

Roll out the dough to ½ cm thick and use a gingerbread boy biscuit cutter to shape the biscuits. Make faces with icing sugar, sultanas and chocolate drops, or leave undecorated.

Bake at 160° C until a delicate golden brown, for approximately 10 to 12 minutes.

The spices in these biscuits make them wonderfully flavourful, and they satisfy childish cannibalistic tastes.

....

After the Wedding

I watched her eyes, horizontal blades of spring grass, half-closed and heavy lidded, as though she'd recently left his bed. I liked her eyes, even as they grew wide and hollow like empty teacups as she took us in, lying in bits and pieces, like broken dolls on a rubbish heap.

She closed the door but not before dropping that tattletale key into a brown blood-puddle. Poor thing. Her story was written the day of their wedding. I knew the anguished hours she would spend trying to clean the key and her mind of the blood. Trying to make excuses for herself and him. I'd done much the same. Only I'd walked deeper into the room, hypnotised by a waxen face that mirrored mine, a sister-me who had already committed the crime of disobeying him. The icy breeze that often played through the rooms of the house followed me into the blood-soaked room and waved the dark curls of my torso-less twin about, like a finicky hairdresser.

I fled in my mind but my body, already awkward with child, and my white satin slippers, betrayed me. I fell, belly first, into brown smears of rusted powder. It stained the key and the white silk dress he'd made me wear every day since I told him of the pregnancy. Soon I joined my co-wives; our stories all the same, all different.

When the door opened, my spirit sighed with sadness. He always made us mute witnesses to his murders. Some he killed swiftly, some he mutilated while their broken bodies still breathed.

She walked into the room first, her torch-eyes lighting the gloom for the others who dragged his beaten body behind them like a carcass. While he accounted for his crimes the men stared at our naked limbs with a revulsion that brought a blistering blush to my chilly cheeks.

She and another, whom she called sister, touched our rigid flesh with capable white hands, washed our skin with sun-warmed water, cleansed us of caked blood stains, encrusted imperfections, and unwanted maggots. Then they matched our limbs, fingers, toes, heads and torsos like human pieces of a jigsaw puzzle, and wrapped each piece in soft, red velvet shrouds. And as we were made whole, bone to bone, he was minced by the men who locked his sentient remains in our former burial chamber with his glowing red key.

She visits our graves; we are not forgotten. We live on through her.

Ringing in the New

THE PHONE RINGS, BUT SHE CANNOT BRING herself to answer it. It looks and sounds sinister, foreign. Everything seems different now, yet she's been away a mere two weeks. When she blinks she expects to see the clinic bedroom, all cheery, non-intrusive colours, but instead she's in her perfect kitchen, with its marbled counter-tops and steel appliances. There are the framed photographs of her sons next to the coffee machine, and there is the phone which won't stop ringing.

Who could be calling her? It is 8 am. Zuhra will be asleep in her faraway time zone. She cannot get up to answer the phone. She feels like an unsewn dress, held together with straight pins; one false move and the whole fragile structure will fall apart.

The phone stops, abruptly, one ring left hanging in the air, like a question mark.

Maybe it's Zain, checking up on her. He's become uncharacteristically attentive since he convinced himself that she tried to kill him; he sees this as a sign of her devotion. She's heard there are people who view abuse – broken bones, bloody gaping holes where teeth should be – as a sign of love and passion. She sees no romance in violence, nothing tender in watching your skin change colour and waiting for welts to heal.

The phone rings again.

She should answer it, it will bring her closer to the coffee machine. She stands up cautiously, moves over to the phone. It stops ringing.

If it rings again she'll answer it, she promises herself.

She makes her coffee, heaps the grounds into the machine, puts a stick of cinnamon and three cloves for protection into the pot, as Zuhra as taught her, and adds enough water for two cups.

The phone rings again.

As she reaches for it, her right eye twitches, a sign that something good is going to happen.

A stranger's voice asks: "Hello? Is that Salena?"

"Yes."

"You don't know me, but, well, I know you. I'm Daisy."

Daisy. The name means nothing to her. Why would anyone name their daughter after a flower?

"I … I want to talk to you. About Zain."

There is no sinking feeling, just her right eyelid ticking like the hand of the clock she can see stuck at an odd angle on the wall. She'll fix it as soon as the caller hangs up.

'What about Zain?"

"I'm his … well, he's made me pregnant. And we want to get married. But he says that you won't divorce him, he says—"

Salena doesn't wait for her to finish. "He's never asked me for a divorce. But of course I know about his affairs. He's hardly discreet." Salena pauses, takes a deep breath. "I think we should meet. Do you have a pen? I'll give you my address."

Daisy hesitates before answering. "No, that's okay. I know where you live."

Of course she does. Salena remembers calling Zain from Zuhra's home earlier that year. During the stilted conversation Salena had heard a subdued girlish giggle; she'd assumed it was the TV.

Again, Salena stops to examine her body, her emotions. Nothing, just the tick tick ticking of her right eye.

"Okay, shall we say midday?"

Salena smiles at the phone, then walks over to reposition the clock. The call is not a huge surprise. By the time she was pregnant with the twins, Zain's infidelities had become commonplace, another of his character traits to which she adapted. After a brief hunt she finds the Yellow Pages nesting in the cupboard under the sink, and makes herself comfortable with the phone and another cup of coffee.

The woman who arrives on the doorstep is precisely what Salena expected. A young girl with yellow hair and a pinched, glum expression. Such a typically South African Muslim male thing to do. Marry a "fair" wife during apartheid and get a white replacement for her when it's over. Salena almost feels embarrassed on Zain's behalf.

She offers Daisy a glass of lemonade, but she refuses it, nervously twisting the fabric of her skirt in her slight hands with their pale pink polished nails. Ma would approve of her colour choice. She is wearing a white dress, ridiculously virginal. Perhaps Zain bought it. He never did have much taste.

As she invites Daisy to sit down, the locksmith arrives. She excuses herself, lets him in, and gives him her orders.

She goes back to the kitchen, where Daisy is tearing at a tissue and crying silently. Salena feels maternal towards this girl. She takes her in her arms and assures her she will not stand in the way of her marrying Zain. She'll give him a divorce and he will be free to marry Daisy and live happily ever after. She hopes for Daisy's sake that Zain is in her thrall, that he is prepared to give up his familiar comforts. He's never liked change. Not that Salena will give him a choice about the divorce; she's already made an appointment with a lawyer from the Yellow Pages.

Then she invites Daisy up to her bedroom and suggests she pack a suitcase for Zain while she checks on the locksmith.

After Daisy leaves, Salena stands next to the fig tree in the front garden, watching the sun play in its leaves. She catches a glimpse of a chameleon on one of the branches, trying to blend in with the green-brown of his surroundings. For the first time in her life Salena realises she can hang up her cloak.

Sacrifices

He says he won't go down on me anymore; I smell fishy. For the love of Neptune, how else is a mermaid supposed to smell? When I think of what I've endured for him. Drinking the sea-witch's excruciating potion, losing my tongue, giving up the gift of my dazzling singing voice, becoming mute with infatuation of him. My powerfully built tail bartered for puny powerless legs, which are okay for dancing, I suppose, but only you don't care about the excruciating pain.

I never believed her when she said that each tread would be agony, that every step would feel like walking on sharpened swords. But she was right. Other girls got colourful, spongy petals strewn in their paths; I got a lifetime of intangible broken glass beneath my feet. Still, I thought the suffering would be worthwhile. When he married me, I would get a soul.

But now he's got someone else. He calls her his little flower, and he wants to marry her. What's special about flowers anyway? They can't sing, they can't swim, they wither without sunlight and they don't have souls. Yet, it's the decorative blossom he wants, not the mermaid who has surrendered everything for him: family, voice, the ability to breathe under water.

Well, two can play at this game. My grandmother always used to tell my sisters and me, when we were hungry, "There's plenty of seaweed in the sea." My sisters, my lovely kind-hearted siblings, have renegotiated the contract with the sea-hag. In exchange for their striking tresses, she's given me a few days to find another man. She says any man will do, they've all got souls. I'm not so sure about that.

I was scrutinising the waves the next dawn, after another night spent alone, watching them change shades from the silvery sleekness of my eldest sister's scales on the tip of her muscular tail to the sapphire of my grandmother's sparkling eyes. He was standing behind me, fishing rod slung over one shoulder, but he looked in my eyes when he asked me if I was unwell, unlike Prince-jerk, who never raised his gaze above my cleavage.

He married me and willingly offered up part of his soul. He bought me bottles of sparkling mineral water and topped them up with sea-salt whenever I looked a little dehydrated. We swam together every evening. He wasn't blind to my pain. He purchased a motorised wheelchair, and one of those computer-operated voices. I was no longer inexpressive. He listened to my words, as if they were the pearls my granny cultivated in her secret oyster garden. He said my stories were his treasure. He reminded me I was a princess; I could do as I pleased. And I did.

Free Strokes

SALENA HAS NOT BEEN TO THE BEACH OR NEAR A POOL since Makeen's death, twenty-three years ago, although often she has dreams in which she is drowning. The salty smell, the crashing waves, remind her of sadness and darkness, of waiting on Woodstock beach for her mother or brother to tell her it was safe to come home.

Now she sits surrounded by sand, sipping iced water from her flask, covered in lashings of Factor 60, watching David, her driving instructor cum lover, swimming out beyond the breakers. Already the sand is creeping into her bathing costume, and she shifts uncomfortably, envisioning the sandy residue that will be left in her washing machine after she's done the laundry. She wonders what her mother would think of her sitting in a backless bathing costume at her age, waiting for a man who is not her husband. She thinks about Ma often, more so now that she's dead than when she was alive. Zuhra says Ma is doing fine; she's probably torturing Papa and haunting Aunty Polla every Thursday night.

It is midday and the white beach stretches in front of her toes for a hundred sandy metres before joining the sea. She watches David stand up in the water, shake the excess drops from his curly hair like a puppy and search out the spot where she is sitting, with a slight frown. His eyes find hers and he gestures for her to join him.

At the water's edge, she hesitates, walks in carefully – a cat who does not wish to wet her paws. A wave surprises her, rushes up to her knees, licks at her costume. David puts his steadying arms around her, hugs her to his wet body, and she shivers with cold and pleasure.

The driving lessons had begun horribly. What was the difference between first gear and reverse? The Golf would shudder and jerk, backwards and forwards, reminding her of sex with Zain. The night after her first lesson she dreamt she was perched in the Golf at the top of a steep hill. The car began to roll down the hill, gently at first, then picking up speed. She could not stop it. She had forgotten which foot went on the brake, the clutch, the accelerator, but before she could crash, her instructor appeared in the seat next to her and stopped the car.

Although embarrassed, she told David about the dream, and he took her for a drive up a steep road in Bo-Kaap and taught her to juggle, to balance the clutch and the accelerator so that she didn't roll back.

Three lessons later, Salena had learnt to drive a manual car, hills and all. She was elated. At the end of the lesson, she invited David in for a Coke. In the kitchen, she offered him some date biscuits. He stood next to her. She could smell the scent of his skin, see the brown down on his arms, and when his hand accidentally touched hers, she felt a jolt of electricity surge through her body – like a computer booting up.

She felt the slippery ice cube in her hand melting as she rubbed it over and up and down his arm. Salena, who, over the years, had perfected the art of motionless sex, became the predator, pushing him up against the silver double-door fridge. Her body taut from decades of scrubbing shower floors and vacuuming responded with glee to David's intelligent fingers as they explored her skin. She was slick with excitement as his penis pressed up against her belly, probing. He slid in with accuracy, and there was none of Zain's huffing and puffing.

Salena felt like an athlete, each inhalation and exhalation of breath charging the cells of her body with greater power. Her skin tingled, and when he pulled away there was a squelching noise from where the sweat had glued their stomachs and chests together.

After their swim, she sits on the sand, her feet in the water, David idly rubbing her back. She watches the waves as they shift backwards and forwards, and for a moment she sees Makeen moving floppily in the water, smiling back at her.

When they leave, David hands her the keys to his car, a sporty Golf GTI. She hesitates, but he assures her it's easy to drive.

The route curves, winds, dips and then rises through the hills. Salena keeps going straight, her eyes fixed on the road ahead, which appears to be melting in the summer sun, a seductive pool, all-absolving, filled with promise.

Hafsa removes Faruk's clinging hand from her neck, and wraps him in his blanket. He moans once and then snuggles deeper into its woolly warmth. She reverses off the bed, silently, hoping the springs won't creak, holding her breath. He opens one drunk-on-milk-eye, then shuts it again with a murmur.

Salena left a few minutes before, with her daadi, for their morning walk to the park, so she has at least an hour. That should be long enough, according to the woman she'd asked for help. So far, the castor oil and hot baths have not worked. Nor have the carbolic soap douche or the wonderkroon, a Dutch remedy. But she has been assured that this will do the trick.

She's prepared. Everything she needs is hidden under her bed, and she reaches for the blue enamel bowl, the soap, Vaseline, the already unwound metal hanger. She has written down the instructions on a small piece of white paper and she carries this along with the other things into the bathroom, before locking the door behind her.

She places each item on the floor next to the toilet. She reaches for the hanger and rubs the Vaseline over its frame, then positions the bowl on the floor. She shuts the toilet lid, puts her left leg on the seat, and with her right hand inserts the pointed hanger deep into that nameless region of the body, one she has never looked at, never touched before, and twists the hanger. Her eyes water. She will not cry out.

She thinks she hears Faruk, listens, but the house is silent. After Faruk was born, Hanif was adamant. No more children. He had his son, and two children were enough.

She struggles to stand over the blue bowl on the floor. Her legs feel crumbly, and she lies down on the cold floor of the bathroom, pain splitting her in unequal portions. There is a popping sound, a burst clot of blood dribbles from inside of her. She calms herself with the belief that she has missed only a single cycle; the Angel Jibreel has not blown a soul into her womb as yet.

Of course, she was right about the absence of the soul. I'd been loitering around her, waiting for the one-hundred-and-twenty-day milestone to be reached so that I could be fused with my body. Hafsa had removed that option; all that was left for me was to stay on as an observer, to watch Salena and Faruk grow up, and, most surprisingly of all, witness Zuhra smile at me and shrug philosophically as she crawled into a space under our mother's skin.

So here I am, with stories of my own, ready to take on the challenges of life. This time I've taken root in more amiable surroundings. This time, Zuhra won't need to cast a magic spell.

My thanks to:

Anne Schuster, luminous writing guide, and her mighty month-
lies, especially my first gentle readers, Anne Woodborne, Maire
Fisher and Nella Freund. xxx

Fourie Botha who saw plenty in scribbles and said, "Thank You!"

Bronwyn McLennan and her soft (ha!) suggestions on how to make
those scrawls legible.

Gabeba Baderoon, friend-gem, for enthusiastic encouragement and
clotted cream memories.

Azhar: inspired insights and R5 massages.

My inimitable mother, for her enchanting evolution.

SB for funding my indolence, with elasticity.

The R11 gang, Peter Korasie, Moya Paterson and Engela Erasmus,
for sunshine in the winter of that particular year.

Zubeida Gierdien for listening lightly to stories about snags.

Katija Kazie, for initiating the culture of reading in our household.

Nurul-Ayn for sketches, Shibnum for pmt-cds and Aliyah for Coke
Float – love you lots.

Word-Gobbler, blessings for your existence in the woods.

And, of course, to mislaid you.